Contents

1. A short prologue by Sharon — 1
2. Lead author Katie barns — 4
3. Rob — 13
4. Amber 3 — 21
5. Kate — 29
6. Charlie — 39
7. Rachael — 46
8. Georgie — 49
9. Sadie 2 — 56
10. Jessica — 62
11. Chloe — 73
12. Amber — 77
13. Jessica 2 — 87
14. Becky — 90
15. Sharon — 96
16. Amber — 101

Derailed and dispersed volume Three

The sacrifice of virgins

Samuel j white

Copyright © Samuelj white books

All rights reserved.

No portion of this book may be reproduced in any form without written permission from the publisher or author, except as permitted by UK copyright law.

A short prologue by Sharon

Where we left volume two, there were at least one hundred of us sitting in the light of what seemed to be a fire, and we were bound together by some unseen force. There were many people from our group and many from the group of pagans. Amber and Jack were sat a few feet from me and Rob who were attached to Mike and Nicola—Nicola was an old friend of mine in the group of pagans, and we had grown up in care together.

Amber was insistent that I was her mother and Rob was her stepfather, and that her name was Sophie. Jack was also adamant that this was true. I had been hit on the head and knocked unconscious, so maybe they had too.

There wasn't any time to think about this, because that woman who called herself Katherine had come in and started making threats. She was also quite clear that the girl who called herself Sophie and claimed to be my daughter was not Amber. In fact, she was bold enough to say that the whole reason we were there is that she wanted to know where Amber was.

She didn't just want her, whoever these people were, they were willing to kill to get their hands on my young housemate. They didn't just threaten on the orders of the woman Katherine, a man came out of the shadows and slit Mike's throat.

We were helpless to stop it and there was nothing that could be done. Mike died right there next to me and there was to be no bringing him back. He had a girlfriend and had been planning to settle down and have a family. Now he was just a crumpled heap of flesh and bones and blood with no life. His head flopped over onto his knees while that awful woman leered at us, laughing and telling us that another person would die in four minutes if we didn't tell her where Amber was.

'The next person to tell me that they don't know where Amber Spellman is,' she smirked in her overly sweetened tone, '...will die immediately then the countdown will start again'

Nicola looked at me then to Katherine, 'But we don't know Amber Spellman' She protested. Katherine gave her a sharp look and screamed, 'Kill this one!'

A figure shot out of the shadows just like before and Nicola realising her mistake was braced to die when Rob shouted, 'Stop don't kill her!'

'Oh, finally somebody is going to tell me where she is,' she cooed.

'*No!*' Rob dared to shout at her. 'You said the next person to say they didn't know where she was would die. But she didn't say that! She didn't say she doesn't know where Amber Spellman is. She said she didn't know her, or who she is, so by what right are you going to kill her?'

'You have a point' she smirked,

looking over at the tall white man who had stopped

just short of killing Nicola, and she nodded towards Rob casually saying,

'Kill him instead.'

The man was onto Rob in a flash, but there was another shout of '*Wait!*' This time it was from Greg.

'This had better not be a waste of my time, otherwise, you two will die together.' Greg was in a different group to me and was a few feet in front of me with his side on.

'I know where she is?' he told her calmly as another figure emerged from the shadows to my left as though waiting for the command to kill Greg. I hoped he knew what he was doing. Greg was fucked because if he didn't really know where she was, which I was sure he didn't, they would kill him. If he did know where she was and got my Amber killed. I would kill the little weasel myself. Maybe he was just trying bravely to buy us all some time.

'She walks right among us,' he said simply. 'Oh, really my dearie' she beamed, bending her knees and crouching so she could look him in the face. 'I knew one of you sweeties would betray her to me if we killed a few of you, but we thought it might take a few more. Be a poppet and tell me where she is, and you can be the last to die.'

As she spoke the light fell on the figure who had come from the shadows to stand behind Katherine. Those of us who knew Amber gasped, as she walked up to Katherine holding a huge knife which she calmly stuck in Katherine's back. I clearly saw the knife come out of her chest before Amber pulled her around to face her and said, 'Here I am bitch. If you want me dead, go ahead and kill me, I surrender.

Lead author Katie Barns

So, erm... hello and thank you for reading. If you've got this far, you've read volumes one and two. You must have enjoyed it enough to keep you going with this. So, I bet you're reading this and thinking, 'Where on earth is Jessica, and who the flipping hell is Katie?'

Well, Jessie being Jessie has got three kids and quite a sizable business too. On top of that, with the business brain she has in her head she has got herself involved in sorting out this Brexit crap (*No opinions here on in or out*) she's just one of those trying to sort the situation out for us all. So, she has little time to put this book together, so she has asked me to help.

So, you're now thinking that you don't remember a Katie Barns being on the train. Well, I wasn't on it. If you've read the book A Midwinter Night's Dream, you may be wondering if I'm the same Katie Barns from that book and the answer is yes, but that's a different story.

So, if you haven't guessed by now, I was the nurse who was looking after Georgie and apparently, her sister Maggy, but there was some confusion over which was which.

I don't like to be selfish in any way, but to give the story substance, you have to talk a bit about yourself to make your part in it.

I have to say that my emotions are mixed. This is because the events of that night were so tragic for so many people. Yet there were those of us including me whose lives would be changed for the better as a direct result. For me it was meeting Georgie, the lady who would become a great friend and in later years since I gave up nursing, she's been my employer and has given me amazing opportunities.

So, I'm off work sick, which is rare for me. I think the reason Jess asked me to do this was to take my mind off of the fact that I may die. As my lovely sister-in-law says, 'You may feel like shit, but nobody under seventy ever died of the flu.' That saying would have some weight if I had the flu.

I'm quite a contradictory person when it comes to my health. There were the days when I'd give myself a good workout in the gym and nip out for a crafty cigarette somewhere between the bike and the rower. After a long battle with addiction, I finally quit smoking a few years back to save my lungs from cancer. How ironic it is that I

now have a cancer which is unrelated to my former habit.

Luckily, I don't think I'm going to die from it. I'm a forward looker not a backward looker and I see this time off as a time to do something different and spend time with the wife and kids.

Oh, by the way, you did read the last bit right, a woman with a wife and kids. I agree there are many lesbians in this story, but I was a lesbian in the past in other books, so it would be strange if I wasn't in this one.

You're now counting how many gay people are in the story. Well, there's Chris, Becky, Mandy and me that I know of. However, life doesn't put people in boxes because if it did there'd be a disabled person, a foreign person, a black person and a drunk Irish person in this story.

Actually, thinking back, there are three of them here
—Georgie, who is disabled, Sadie, who is foreign and Sammy who's Irish (And used to be drunk but is many years sober). Before people jump on the racism card and start saying there are no black people in the book, There are! you just don't know that you already met them. I would like to add that I lived in Norfolk until I was Twelve and I didn't meet a black person until I moved to Essex. However, in 2020 I live in Norfolk again and find it much more racially diverse.

So, we need to get on to what was going on that night and how I came to be part of it.

I moved away to be with my dad when I was twelve. I moved to be with my dad, because my older sister was not his daughter. This meant she couldn't come with me and had to stay with mum. I hated my older sister Katherine because as a child she'd bully me, not only with words, but she would kick me and burn my hair and force me to cut myself.

I was many things in those days, and a nurse was not one of them. A very good liar was one of those things. I had Georgie and her sister convinced that I was a nurse. In truth, I would be a nurse in the future, but that night I was a sixteen-year-old child, and I was out there, because I was staying with my mum in the school holidays.

So, I said, my mum and my sister were out there, but they were not out there together. My mum was with the pagans who had come to worship the moon, but my sister was not. She was there with some other people. I didn't know the details at the time, but my sister was there for sure.

My sister Katherine is five years older than me. She was, is, and will always be a mad power-hungry woman, wanting control of as many things as she can get. When we were kids, she tried to be the boss of me. At school, she was the head girl because she blackmailed the teachers, and now in her job, she had bullied and blackmailed her way to being a deputy hotel manager at age twenty. She already had the knife ready to stick in her boss's back.

Little did we know that she had blagged her way into a group where she did not belong. I didn't know of these people and the fact that I know now they exist terrifies me. However, what terrifies me more is that my sister was not born into this cult of magic people. They were born to use magic to kill people and they had no choice about that. My sister, however, wanted to join them by choice and it seems that she somehow got them on side. I think she did it in the hope that she could gain her own magic and use it to get more power and control.

Please rest assured that my sister Katherine is now rotting away in jail for a murder she committed nearly nine years after these events. However, she only got twenty years for killing a poor pregnant girl who she shoved down a flight of stairs. In eleven years, she will be out, claiming she was provoked to anyone who will listen.

So, going back to the start of the day. I told Georgie and Maggy I was a trainee nurse, but the truth is I attended a couple of St John's Ambulance meetings with my mum and picked up a bit of knowledge from her. No, really, I was a Sixteen-year-old kid and I finished school the day before, and I got the train up to Norfolk to spend some quality time with my mum over the holidays.

I must say that I have never had a bad relationship with either of my parents despite being over the moon when they split up. Mum couldn't help that Kathy was her daughter. My mum wasn't as strict as my dad. Dad and his new wife brought me up properly in contrast to Mum who saw me more as a friend than a daughter rather than put a stop to my bad habits. She openly let me drink and smoke since I was fourteen in some sad attempt to seem like a cool mum.

I came out that night to spend some quality time with my mum and ended up living in a nightmare. Even the thoughts of what could have happened that night make me want to go and hug my two daughters and all my many nieces and nephews and tell them I will always be here to fight. Then I remember I've got cancer so I can't promise that, because there's always the risk that I don't have a future myself.

A lot of people in the last part of the story told the reader where they were. I might as well explain where I am. I'm at a hotel in Cromer, not the one I work for, the better one owned by my wife's sister and brother-in-law Rob and Kat. I am typing while keeping an eye on the kids as they run around the huge garden.

So, at fifteen I was old enough to stay at home while my mum went to this bloody pagan thing. I could have been sitting home in the warm in front of the TV, drinking my mum's wine and sneaking a few of her cigarettes. However, I thought the pagan thing would be more of a laugh. I thought they were all a bunch of deluded idiots, but they were a nice friendly bunch of idiots.

Plus, most of the hard work had been done by the time I got there, so ironically my first part of the evening while we waited for the moon to show, was to share a bottle of wine and a pack of ciggies with my mother. My mother Jane Barns was quite the hypocrite, she was the head nurse (or Sister) in the main cancer ward at the Norfolk and Norwich hospital giving her daughter boos and flags.

So, we were out in the marshes quite a long way from the road and the railway. Because of the road closures, we had had to walk a few miles to reach the camp. There were several tents already pitched, including the first aid tent, but I had to erect the sleeping tent for my mother and I, seeing as she wasn't very good at stuff like that among other things like parenting. I tease, but really, I adored my mum.

To be fair to my mother though she was a bloody good nurse and did well considering she was nearly fifty years old and working twelve-hour night shifts on little sleep. It was my mum who inspired me to want to be a nurse and I'd done some good first aid training with the Girl Guides when I moved to Essex —which I loved every minute of—however a nurse I was not back then. And to be honest when I was one, I was not a good one like she was.

So, the pagan group were a friendly bunch. I thought they would all be weirdos, but in fact, we all got along famously. I've come to realise in more recent years that I get

along well with weirdos, because I am myself a weirdo, but I just didn't realise it then.

There was loads of us out there, maybe two hundred. Many people had been involved in building a huge fire out in the marshes. It was the biggest fire I have ever seen or will ever see again. It must have taken the people who built it several days and a superhuman effort.

The stack of logs was a long walk from the campsite, let alone the village or the road and railway. Yet it was bigger than your average house. They had built several wicker men, not unlike the one from the 1970s movie where Edward Woodward is killed by pagans. I had joked with them that if they wanted somebody to burn, then my big sister Katherine would be a perfect person to burn.

Some of them apparently knew my sister and agreed with this. I was assured that it was just a celebration of Yule and that the use of wicker men to burn people was propaganda used by the Romans to make the Celts seem frightening.

Before those in the know about these types of things, point out that wicker men are usually used in the spring. Even I know that. I was told by some of the pagans that this year with the blood moon, it was far from the usual celebration and the wicker men were something extra to make this year even better.

Going back to my sister, I had heard she was also out there worshipping the blood moon, but not with these lovely people. She was out there with a different group of people. It was unknown really, whether or not they were a rival group of pagans or just a bunch of drunken idiots who thought they could do magic.

I had no idea what was waiting out there in the dark.

Even then at such a young age, despite my bad habits and my rough upbringing in the early years, since living with my dad, I had learnt to be a self-confident young woman. I think those who know me will say despite me being laid back and a little nervous; I do end up being the life and soul of the party once I feel comfortable. I've grown to be very charismatic as my wife puts it and I go out of my way to make friends with everyone. You know the type of person I am. For example, if we're at the same party and don't know each other and you haven't said hello to me, you bet I'll be the one to say hello to you.

I was making lots of new friends, that's what I think I'm trying to say. So, there were a huge lot of us sat around a medium fire, drinking the most wonderful coffee which we boiled on the fire in a huge cauldron-like pot. As a group we consumed enough caffeine to keep us up until sunrise. I remember watching the train making its way across the marsh on the way to Great Yarmouth as I sat in my camp chair by the fire with my feet up, wondering who would be going to bloody shitty Yarmouth at this time of night. I also wondered who would be leaving Yarmouth on that train and why they had gone there at all, let alone left it so late to go home—Great Yarmouth is not my favourite place in the world.

I also noticed as some people sat there in their ceremonial clothes, putting their face paint on as we drank our coffee, that so many people had sniffly colds.

I'd never heard so many sniffs and sneezes and nose blowing around me. I kind of wondered if this was a fast-spreading cold that the group was sharing with each other. I had been feeling in top health—for a fifteen-year-old who drank and regularly smoked despite being good at sports—but soon after arriving I came down with a blocked nose and heavy cough like many of the others.

Seeing the train had reached Great Yarmouth, I noticed some movement from the distance. There were lights coming from the direction of where the other people, including my sister, were camped. I wondered if it was some music festival, or something going on, not that I wanted to go. However, I had heard from members of our group that the other camp was not friendly and that they warned there would be violence if any of us entered their camp. I assumed that my sister Katherine was behind those threats. She was a horrible bitch and even my mother agreed.

The light from their camp was building as it seemed that several of them had flame torches burning like members of our group, but they were too far away to tell. I had no idea at this time how many of them there were or who they really were.

While we waited to light our big fire, theirs was already alight and despite them being very far away we could hear chanting and shouting from their camp. They must have outnumbered us by many to make that sort of noise.

Several of us saw bright lights coming from their camp, shooting like a giant fireworks into the sky in the direction of the railway. Even though the tracks were a good two miles away, the fireworks seemed to reach the very area where the train had just passed. There were a few groans from our group suggesting their displeasure at this kind of behaviour putting the lives of the people on the train in danger.

I thought nothing more of it and decided to have a go at helping some of the ladies put on their face paint. It must have been around 10:15 p.m., when out of nothing the earth shuddered and threw several of us off our feet including me.

Looking around and picking each other up, I heard people shouting screaming and pointing to the railway, where we could see fire.

There were not many words as we gazed around at each other. My mum said nothing and picked up her first aid kit and grabbed my arm as though to tell me I was coming with her as I stood there with my mouth open and heart racing.

Just because my mother was a nurse and I'd been a cadet, this didn't mean we were the only people who knew first aid. There was a group of around fifteen of us that marched off at a lung-bursting pace through the freezing mud.

We'd been walking only five to ten minutes when the second explosion sent fire into the sky and burned our ears.

Obviously, you already know that I never reached the train, but when the second explosion hit, we began to run as fast as we could —which was not very fast.

We seemed to get ever closer to the train when one of the guys at the lead of the group fell to the ground with a shout. What he had tripped on was one of the two young women. We immediately stopped and checked them over to find that both was still breathing.

So, the obvious thought in all of our heads, was what were these two girls doing out here? They were a long way from the train. How did they get to be unconscious? The more important thing, however, was to get them off of the wet floor and get them somewhere where we could help them.

We had two beds set up in the first aid tent in case of emergencies and my mum directed a few of us to take these two there once we had made sure they had no injuries that would be made worse by carrying them without a stretcher.

In the torchlight, I could see that both of the women were very similar looking. They were skinny and pretty with dark hair. Even in the torchlight, it was clear to me that these were identical twins. One of them, however, was missing a leg and had a pair of crutches, but it soon became clear that the leg she did have was prosthetic. Her leg was not one of those mechanical-looking ones or the blades that the Paralympians use. It didn't look like an NHS one either. It looked bloody expensive which led to the question, where was her other leg?

There wasn't any time to lose, because the people on the train needed help, so my mum headed off in that direction leaving four of us to take the two ladies back to the tent. Once at the tent the other three would go for help while I kept watch over these two ladies and checked their obs and treated them for both shock and hypothermia.

Usually, I joke with people and tell them I'm a small,

weak woman and I can't carry things. However, in this situation, I did what I could and helped to carry the girl with a missing leg. It was quite awkward carrying her and her crutches as she was unconscious, and she was a dead weight. The others who were carrying her sister also struggled.

Although both girls were breathing and stirring as we carried them, neither of them woke up. I could only imagine what sort of casualties were at the train. I wished I could have been there to help. With my mother on the way, I knew they had one of the best nurses around. My mother may not have been a great parent or example of health and fitness, but she was the head nurse on her ward at the Norfolk and Norwich Hospital, so she was one of the best people to be there.

My mother's last words to me as she turned towards the train seeing that I was having a crisis of confidence, were to tell me to put her uniform on and pretend to be a nurse, then people would not question me. 'Do what you do well.' She smiled, 'Fake confidence and bluff your way through it like you do everything else.'

I didn't know as I walked to help these two girls, that I would never see my mother again.

Rob

I must admit that I was confused by a lot of things. I don't or didn't believe in magic or anything like that. As I mentioned earlier, I was in the band Rock Corn Storm. During my time in the band, there were a lot of dark themes used on our album covers, fantasy art that sort of thing. There were monsters and the like on the cover with a sort of bat-out-of-hell style.

During the shows, lead singer Lizzy would often dress up as a witch for a bit of fun and I could often be seen playing the bass with devil's horns.

That was in the days when we were all friends without egos and music was still fun.

So, witches, wizards, god, the devil and that was made up. My father always told me that he believed this crap was all made up by the church in medieval times to scare simple people into the church on Sundays. Once people are in the church the vicar and the leaders of the church from high society then have a hold over the poor people.

If you look into history and meanings, the word witch, means wise woman. Most villages had a wise women who actually used there knowledge to help people. It was, in fact, the church in 1600 who victimised these people and turned the population against them with ridiculous claims and made them victims of hate.

Ghosts as well, I was always told that these stories were made up to keep people in their houses. Black Shuck is supposedly a big black dog that takes your soul away. There was a church in North Norfolk where Black Shuck, the dog of the devil trapped the parishioners inside while he terrorised them with his fiery breath.

Black Shuck was the inspiration for the Hound of the Baskervilles and made Sir Arthur Conan Doyle a lot of money. However, the real origins of the tale came from the smugglers who frequented the shores of Norfolk. What better way to scare the locals into staying away from the coast while they were up to their lawbreaking and not wanting to be caught.

So, in my mind, it was all a bit of fun. People like to be scared by stories. They entertain people and make them forget about how boring and risk-free everyday life is. Who wouldn't want to go to Narnia and fight the White Witch, instead of going to work in an office? Who wouldn't want to go to Hogwarts rather than a public secondary school in Colchester where people do drugs on the back of the toilet?

So, you can imagine my surprise when the witches turned out to be real. They were not true witches in the sense that they were not like the wise women who were persecuted in the 1600s. These people had the power to just point their finger at something and make it happen without traditional wands or broomsticks used in many stories.

What the group of people we met out on the marsh before we were set upon had told us was true. They may have been pagans, but they were peaceful. Despite paganism and witchcraft being very similar, if not the same.

Sharon had been knocked out, so her account of what happened in the lead up to Mike's murder cannot possibly tell everything.

I was awake the whole time. The group chasing us contained things that I had never seen the likes of before and probably never will again. There were monsters the size of houses with feet the size of cars. They had huge scales and horns. Then I'm pretty sure a minotaur, a flying horse and several huge dogs were present.

Some of them used very human weapons on us like bats and knives and their fighting skills were super-human and far too much for unarmed people. Sharon was hit on the back of the head and knocked out cold, but I caught her.

There were far too many of them to fight and we were soon caught in the middle of a circle. Our little group and the peaceful pagans made around one hundred people. We were in the middle with the witches, wizards and monsters trapping us around the outside holding us hostage.

After a few moments of trying to fight them without knowing what the hell we were doing, it was clear we hadn't got a chance of getting away. They obviously had magic on their side. I suddenly felt my arms lock to Mike, and Nicola and they in turn seemed to both be locked to Sharon, who was still out cold. Very soon we were all in groups of four.

There was panic and screaming everywhere as you would expect, but then it all went silent.

The silence was because we were all stiff as boards.

Still alive and conscious inside, but not able to move on the outside. I could see and hear everything that went on but could not so much as twitch a finger. All the others were the same, like living statues in real clothes.

Out of the sky shone a bright light, it was almost like stage lighting shining on the group of us in the middle. For a moment I was reminded of being back on stage with the band. However, if my eyes were to be believed, there was this woman who seemed to float effortlessly out of the crowd as they cheered her. When she reached the centre of the group, she stopped dead and the crowd around us bowed down to her on their knees.

Whoever this woman was, she was old and looked quite frail. The skin on her face as she walked around looking at the group was saggy, and her hair was white and wispy.

Despite having floated into the group, she looked like she may have been well into her nineties. You could hear a pin drop as she walked around. In front of me, she stopped, and she took a handkerchief from her old tatty clothes and blew her nose. Then she took a deep sniff and continued to walk around us, sniffing hard at everyone.

After a while, she put up her head and frowned before addressing her group. 'Fools,' she sneered 'You have been fooled. There is not a single whiff of virginity in this group of people.'

Her tone was one of anger not at us, but at her own kind. 'You people had three tasks, one to kidnap a pregnant woman, two, to bring me the two virgins who were on the train, and three, not to be seen.' Her voice echoed through the darkness. 'You have failed at all three tasks.'

There was a deadly silence as the woman looked around angrily. 'Come on people,' she cried 'I have other things to do to prepare for the end of the world. There are thousands of you and only one of me. I'm four hundred years old! Must I do everything?'

Everything was going around in my head—witches and magic are real. This woman is trying to prepare for the end of the world, and she is four hundred years old. She wanted two virgins and a pregnant woman from the train. She was talking about people from our train. Kate was pregnant so she must have meant her, then there were two virgins. If there were any virgins in our group, not meaning to be personal, that might have explained why Georgie was missing. They must have got her.

I didn't mean any offence to Georgie, saying I thought she was a virgin, but I just didn't think she was physically able, or willing seeing as she turned down offers from a lot of guys. One of them being me when I was drunk, I think (Sorry Georgie)—she made the right choice there—but moving on.

The other one was Greg, no offence again to Greg, but surely nobody was ever drunk enough to have sex with Greg. However, this woman was using her senses to smell virgins, but she must have been mistaken as Greg was only a few feet from me.

You couldn't make up a dream like this, honestly. There I was planning to go home from work and get an early night. I was supposed to be picking up my daughters from their mum in the morning. A train crash is one thing but sitting out in a field with a load of strangers while a woman who claims to be four hundred years old and seems to lead an army of magical creatures sniffs us to see if we are virgins. Seriously? My soon-to-be ex-wife wasn't going to take that as an excuse if I was late.

Even back when I had my five minutes of fame, I had only taken drugs a few times, and even on LSD I never saw shit like this.

'I hear that the pregnant slut is still at the train,' The old woman told the crowd. 'Why don't some of you morons toddle off and catch her before help reaches her, while I give these prisoners a little magic.'

By her reaction, some of the group must have gone to find the pregnant girl, who I assumed was Kate.

'So human beings,' she said with a smile breaking out across her face, addressing the hundred or so of us that were under the spell which had stopped us from moving. 'There are one hundred, and twenty-two of you sitting here, and another hundred or so locked up a mile away and there is not one virgin among you.'

'Let's have some fun while we wait for the baby snatchers,' she said leering in my direction. 'If you don't want to see any magic put your hand up.'

Obviously, nobody could do that because we were all stuck in the same position.

'Oh goody, I do love a show,' she leered, the watching crowd cheered her little joke.

'Okay.' She smiled. 'Let's have a little look around.' She came to one of the pagans and pointed a finger down at her and said, 'Your name is Lisa Bradfield, thirty-six, you're married with two little boys who are at home with your husband, who doesn't believe in your religion, but he is fine with you being here tonight. However,...' she teased. '...what he doesn't know is that while you go on these little overnight outings, you are having sex with... this young lady over here.'

With that, she pointed right at Nicola, the woman who Sharon knew. Then moving in that direction, she continued to Sharon who, apparently, remembers none of this, but I do have her permission to say.

'Oh, now we have an interesting case. Sharon Carter, thirty-two, likes to pretend she spreads herself a bit thin when she hasn't even had sex with anyone.'

A thought crossed my mind, and in a flash, the woman had read my mind and she responded 'Oh yes, dear, that would be correct. If she has not had sex, then she is the virgin I need, but alas no. Sharon here was raped when she was a child.'

I was shocked and upset if this was true about Sharon, though it would certainly explain a few things about the poor woman.

The old woman smelt her again and laughed. There was a roar of laughter from the crowd that made me want to be sick, and the roar got louder when the old woman announced that Sharon had a child who was taken from her. 'Seventeen years old and she still can't find the girl who lives so close.'

'Who's the father of the child I wonder?' She asked the crowd with a leer towards me as she read my own disgusted thoughts.

She stopped close to me with putrid breath, and she bent over Sharon as though taking a look into her soul. A smile came across her face with a laugh of evil like I'd never seen. She looked as though she'd just heard the funniest joke ever told and was going to laugh herself to death like the Monty python sketch. I thought she might fall down dead with laughter and hoped she would.

Finally, she staggered to her feet holding her chest breathing calmingly in and out as the crowd waited to here what was so funny.

'The rapist of this poor sweet innocent woman.' She wheezed trying to compose herself before taking a deep calming breath. 'Was a children's social worker called Michael Baker. Or at least he was then known by that name at the time. He's now known by another name Peter Spelman.'

I couldn't see what was funny and I felt terrible for Sharon and what she went through without this public humiliation.

'What is funny young man' She added looking at me barely able to hold herself. 'Is that her rapist is my own grandson.'

I wanted to shout and scream at her that rape is a horrible act that no woman or man of any age should have to be put through. I didn't even have breath in my lungs. Thank the stars that Sharon was out cold and never got to hear these horrors.

It was not her place to be saying these things to everyone, Sharon was a person and not something to be made fun of.

'There's one more thing before we go,' she smiled coming to me. 'You're her idol. She was at every one of your band's shows. She still has your picture on her bedroom wall, and she still lusts after you, despite the fact she barely speaks to you. You have much that you deny, but you my man, are still in love with your ex-wife. An ex-wife who, if I have my facts right, still loves you and wishes that she had not left you and wants to give things another go.'

I didn't like her talking about my life either. My marriage to my ex-wife was over, but we had stayed good friends, and maybe she was right, and things were saveable still, but how could a stranger know these things. And wait…… Sharon was at my shows and still had a picture of me on her wall and fancied me. Seriously?

'Shame…' she smiled '…seeing as you're going to die tonight, it doesn't look like you're going to get that happy ending, does it?'

Another roar came from the horrible crowd.

'Ohh...' she said suddenly, '...I hear they've got the pregnant girl and the father trapped and they're on their way. I think it's time for a proper magic trick to please the crowd.'

She stood right in front of me and reached into her tattered old cloak and took out what looked like a weird crack pipe, lighting it with a spark from the tip of her finger.

The pipe burned red, and the old woman looked at it glowing and admired it for a moment. 'It's genetically modified for my own smoking needs.'

I can never unsee what I saw next. The old woman's clothes disappeared, and she stood there in front of me with haggard and wrinkled skin and boobs down to her waist. You don't even want to know what I saw below her waist, because the thought of it makes me want to be sick.

I don't want to offend old people, but she looked like a rotting corpse. If I was physically able to be sick at that point, I would have been.

She continued as she held the pipe up to her mouth. 'let's see if their little human minds explode when I do this.' With that, she took a deep drag and the pipe glowed even brighter as she breathed it in.

As she breathed in the smoke, the woman's eyes widened and something about her face was changing, when she exhaled and disappeared behind a cloud of red smoke. After two further puffs of red smoke wafted into the air, she knocked out the pipe.

When the red smoke cleared there in the place where the old woman had stood with her wrinkles and her white hair, stood somebody completely different.

This woman was also naked, but she was young, slim, and toned. She had a stunning face and an even better body and a main of shining red hair to go with it. I think this sudden newcomer was the second most stunning woman I have ever seen. The one who beat her to first place is my wife, and I'm saying that, so I don't get a slap when she reads this.

It was only when I saw the pipe still in her hand and heard her voice that I realised what the old woman's trick had been.

'Well,' she said, beaming. 'They tell me smoking is bad for you, but it seems to have made me eighteen again.'

There was another tremendous roar of applause from the waiting crowd.

'Somebodies got a boner' she mocked.

'Now,' she continued, addressing the crowd of her own kind once again. 'I have a baby to steal. Good news! I hear we have the boy virgin imprisoned in camp. The girl, wherever she is, will find this out and by the time we need her, I believe she will come to us in a useless attempt to free her little friends.'

Clothes appeared on the body of the now- young lady as she concluded her speech with instructions to the crowd to take us to their base.

As she vanished into the night, I felt myself still stiff as a board, but floating now high in the air. I saw the others, all still motionless statues, floating with me. Then, with a whoosh, the group of us seemed to travel over a mile in less than a second before being dropped to the ground, where the statue spell was released. We were, however, still magically handcuffed to each other.

That was about where we were when Sharon woke up at the end of part two. The bit where she described, two young people looking and sounding like Amber and Jack claiming that I was married to Sharon, and that the girl Sophie was her daughter. Then another horrible twisted evil woman, this time called Katherine had addressed us asking for us to turn in the real Amber.

I don't want to go over Mike's death any further, and the prologue of this book explained how Amber heroically appeared out of the shadows and offered her life for ours.

I remember there were looks of confusion from a lot of people. This might have been because many of them didn't know who she was. However, there were shocked cheers when people saw that she had put a Knife in the back of Katherine.

Unfortunately, Katherine didn't die and made a full recovery. Before any of us could communicate to poor Amber, she was set upon by the witches and wizards from the crowd. As she was being dragged away, I heard her scream to her capturers 'Now you've got what you want you can let the others go.'

However, her cries for a bargain fell on deaf ears as the crowd of several roared and chanted, 'Your gonna burn in a minute. You're gonna burn in a minute.'

It was like the end of a second-rate movie. The 'all is lost' moment where nothing can seemingly be done to save the situation. I may not have known Amber well or liked much about what I did know about her. I certainly was wrong about her. She had offered her own life so we could live.

Amber 3

I wasn't meant to be in this volume. My story was meant to be resolved in part four, but this volume was a little short of content because Georgie has bailed on us. Bless her, she felt awful about leaving us in the lurch, but she had to go somewhere very far away on business, and for a long time.

She's doing some charity work in Africa. I wouldn't put it past her to be using her dad's money to do something good in the world. She'll kill me for saying this because she doesn't like to take credit, but she has funded the building of several schools out in the third world. I wouldn't be surprised if she was putting her millions into building a spaceship to fly the starving children to Mars to start a better life or something. We all love her. Basically, she went somewhere where she couldn't email her story to the rest of us, so I have stepped in, and it all got rearranged to tie in.

So, Katie and Jess have asked me to write my part here. Me being me, I've told them, 'No, thank you. I'm too busy at the moment.'

To be fair I am running two businesses, so they gave me some slack. Then after a few weeks, they started leaning on me and nudging me again, to which I asked them, 'Would you ladies, please stop leaning on me while I'm at work? I'm trying to serve customers.' Luckily, they were the customers I was trying to serve.

I suppose the real reason I haven't got on and done this earlier was that the last two volumes left me emotionally drained. The time between should have helped me recover, but instead, it made me worse. I've visited some of the dark places and spaces that I know well from my days as a teenager, struggling with depression. The relapse came as somewhat of a shock to me, as I've been so happy for so long.

It's not just the past, but the present that has caused it to return. But I'm on the mend now, some way back to being the happy me.

Luckily for me I have a huge network of support and managed to stay away from old nicotine and alcohol habits, but I must admit I'm being heavily supported by the others in the group. Maybe it's because they realised. I'm not as bad as everyone thought I was and that my bark and my bite are very different things.

I'm also the baby of the group. Yes, you heard that right! I will be thirty-eight years old this summer and my kids are older than I was that night twenty years ago, but I will always be the baby even in my Fifties.

So, go back a few sentences… Now you're thinking what…? Is this the same person who was crying and trying to kill herself earlier in the story because she had no ovaries and couldn't have a baby. Adoption is probably your first thought, but one look at my big pregnant belly I'm sporting right now would change your mind.

Well now you must think that the doctors had got things wrong, but they didn't. Am I a walking talking miracle? Well, I don't like blowing my own trumpet, so I will just say that, yes, I am, and we will leave it at that. What have my pregnancy and my older kids got to do with this story? Well, everything really.

So, I better move on with the story. As usual, I am going to tell you where I'm writing from. I'm not far from where I was before when I sat outside on the pub bench where I sat when I was seventeen.

I now part own the pub, so I can sit where I like. Instead of on the bench, I'm inside in a comfy seat where I can still look out of the window over the harbour. It's raining out, so if I went out, I'd get the laptop wet, and my glasses steamed up.

Yes, glasses. I may look and act like I'm still in my twenties or younger, but reading glasses are the giveaway that I'm getting old. Never mind, my nineteen-year-old daughter being more pregnant than me. (I'm gonna be a granny) My writing snacks include a pot of tea and some grapes. I'm prepared with a hanky too, knowing that I might need to dry my eyes at some point in the writing. I'm not saying that you as a reader are going to cry, but for me these memories still sting like hell.

They sting like hell because of Jack or… well, because of the current absence of Jack, my best friend can't be here with us anymore.

One of the things that gets to me is that if I would have arrived just a few minutes earlier, Mike would be alive. His girlfriend and his family wouldn't have had to go through all the shit they did. I can't bear to think what would happen if I lost one of my kids and knowing that I may have been able to help to stop them losing theirs breaks me.

I wish to god that I could say that I had killed that evil bitch when I stabbed her, but I know for a fact that she lived and she is finally where she belongs, rotting in jail for a different crime she committed some years later.

Well, questions that remain up to that point are as follows. How did I know they needed me? How did I know where they were? How did I know where to find them? And last, but not least, why? Why did I go there knowing that my death would not only be the end of me, but maybe the end of the world as we know it?

Well, the world as I knew it was already gone, to be fair. Trolls existed, so either I banged my head, or the world was already fucked. If an eighty-to-one-hundred-foot-tall troll existed, then who was I to argue with him about these witches that he said were trying to take over the world?

I remembered him though now that he said. Naturally, when he saved me from falling as a child, I thought I was dreaming, but here he was, and he knew me and wanted to keep me safe.

But even in your wildest fantasies, you don't think of a troll as being as big as him. I mean, what on earth sort of bridge were the Billy goats walking over if he could fit under it?

The Humber Bridge, or maybe the Golden Gate Bridge may accommodate his size, but the whole world would have known he was there. I would have described him as more of a giant, but that would imply he was a big human, but he wasn't. He had scales and big pointy ears, claws and foul-smelling breath. Something about him made me think of a scaly Cat.

So, if you have read volume two, you will know he told me about these people trying to use the blood moon to raise the devil and he told me they needed a virgin to help, and I was one of two virgins on the marsh that night.

The other virgin was not Gregory as I first thought. I would apologise to Greg for saying that but I'm not going to because it's him and I do love him, really.

Instead, it was my childhood friend Jack, and worst of all they had caught him

Now I knew the whole world was at stake. If what he said was right and I knew my friendship with Jack had been strained of late, due to me not wanting to be his girlfriend —which I actually did want, but it couldn't happen.

My feelings were still a bit selfish at that point. If me going to save my best friend was going to put the whole world at risk of being destroyed. So, my decision was to say, 'FUCK you guys. I'm gonna save Jack and if I fail and the world ends, then so be it. You never know I might just have saved both.

So, where we left it, I had escaped the prison I was placed in by Ulskane the troll. I was fit, I'd been going out for runs in an effort to get healthy. So, obviously in my mind I was a top-class athlete who could outrun a giant troll. In reality, I was still a little overweight, and yes, I worked out, but I also drank, smoked and ate McDonalds multiple times a week. He let me get about a hundred metres before casually picking me up in one hand.

'Let me go!' I screamed, breathing hard with sweat already starting to form on my face as I kicked and fought in vain. He pulled me up close to his face. 'Shush, Amber, I have to keep you safe. They're going to hear us or see us.'

'I don't care!' My voice echoed into the night as he lifted me high into the sky. 'I didn't want to live in this world before tonight, I definitely don't want to live in it now I've heard about all this paranormal shit.'

'Calm, please.' He breathed, holding me so close to his face that his putrid breath filled my lungs, causing me to choke so hard it brought tears to my eyes. If anyone was watching, it must have looked like a seen from King Kong with the beast holding the beautiful woman in his hand. Well, it would have done if it wasn't me, because I'm hardly Fay Wray, Naomi Watts, or Bree Larson, but you get the gist.

'If you don't care, why are you running? Don't you trust me?' He boomed in an attempted whisper.

'I want to save Jack!' I cried. 'If I don't do anything he'll die, and he doesn't deserve it, and nor does anyone. Despite everything I do all the time, I've been a giant pain in the ass. He has always been my friend and stood by me and he deserves better than this.'

'That sounds to me like a person who cares,' he breathed. Tears rolled down my face as I took a deep rattling attempt at a calming breath.

'I care,' I sobbed. 'I care about Jack, about Sharon and Jessie and Mandy. God, I even care about those shitty awful people who called themselves my parents. I can't watch them grow old and have families knowing that I'm an empty broken body who can't have the one thing I've always wanted. If I can find a way to save Jack and the others from whatever's out there, then I'll save them. If I die trying, then so what? Who gives a fuck about grumpy shitty Amber Spellman?'

'As I told you,' he growled, but not menacingly. 'If you are not successful in saving the boy, they will catch you and kill you both and your death could bring about the destruction of the entire human race. Now shut up and hide.'

'No,' I screamed. 'No, I have to save Jack.'

'Do you think your friend would want you to risk the lives of everyone on the planet to save him.' He bellowed, suddenly forgetting that he was trying to stay quiet. I stopped, silent, speechless, not knowing what to do. I wanted to go for Jack, even if I just got the briefest second to tell him that I loved him. Explain that I always had and why I pretended not to. But if the troll was right, then just doing that could put the whole human race at risk.

Of course, I was still sceptical of everything the troll had said. Surely, Jack and I were not the only virgins out there that night. Then there was the whole thing about the fate of the human race? That's very high stakes. It sounded like the plot of a TV show or something from Hollywood, and not something that goes on in Norfolk. Yet I didn't have the choice to believe it, because I was talking to a troll. An hour ago, I was going to walk up the rails and throw myself under the train, and if I had done so I would have died none the wiser to this world he spoke about within our own.

He was already striding back towards the old wind pump where he had captured me, holding me down by his side in his tight grip. Even if I did want to risk the fate of humans just to see Jack one last time, there was no way that

I could escape him. There were so many things rattling around in my head. Usually when mulling over things in my head I would sit back in a comfy chair with a big cup of coffee and a roll up and have a good think. However, that old wind pump was not exactly equip with an armchair and coffee machine. I had to sort out the mess in my head and quickly.

What if the troll was lying? What if these bad people did not exist? I saw no evidence of them. What if he was the cause of the train crash and this whole story about devil worshipers was made up? But if I couldn't get away from him, I would never know he was really trying to protect me from them, or if he had kidnapped me for his own purposes. Then something hit me. It was an idea of such utter brilliance that I'm still proud of myself now for thinking of it.

'Kill me,' I breathed. He stopped and held me up to his face again so I could see the yellow of his eyes and breathed, 'What?'

I took a few trembling breaths and repeated in a much higher voice. 'Kill me.'

The troll said nothing and with only the light of the moon and the stars to see his face by, I could not read his expression. I'm not good at reading expressions of humans in the light, let alone trolls in the dark. After a moment though, he spoke slowly. 'Why would you ask me to end your life child?'

I felt his tight grip on me release enough for me to wipe my eyes on my sleeve. 'If what you say is true.' I trembled, sobbing. 'If these people exist and they need me to complete their awful spell, why don't we just take away one of the things they need.' I paused and took a deep sniff, wishing I hadn't dropped Jessie's hanky. 'They can't use me for the spell if there is no me. So, if you kill me, then that's that right?

They can search these marshes and beyond, and even if they find me, they can't sacrifice somebody who's already dead?'

Again, he was silent for a moment. The sound of his breathing and my crying was only a whisper on the wind. If everything he told me was true, he would have listened to me, and killing me would be for the best.

'If what you told me is true, you must kill me.' I shivered. 'But if you don't kill me, I will have to assume you're lying to me, and keeping me alive is for your own gain. But if I am going to die tonight whatever happens the world won't miss me so if you want to keep them from finding me, do it.'

'Sophie Spellman, you are one of a kind.' He groaned. 'You consider yourself a dumb blonde. But in that tiny head of yours, you have more intelligence than my kind can ever possess, and you are right. If I was to kill you now, it would bring an end to this.' He paused from speaking and released me from his grip, letting me step onto the ground. He bent low so that he could look down at me.

Shakily I took out my cigarette lighter, so he could see my face and see that I was saying it in earnest. I took out a pre-rolled cigarette and put it in my mouth. I don't know why but I'd seen it somewhere on tv or something. Smoking before you're about to die puts you at ease.

'You're sure?' he asked as gently as he could. I nodded although part of me was wondering if I was. 'What if I was just testing to see if he would go through with it.' If he did, I could yell at him to stop, and I would know he was telling the truth and we could find a way around this. If he did, then I would die, and it would all be over anyway.

'Crush me.' I shivered. 'Do it quickly. Stamp on me and get it over with. And when I am gone you take my place and you go and save my Jack for me, and you tell him I didn't love him, even though we both know I'd sell my soul for him, and make sure he moves on and he's happy. And you save the others, and you tell them I died for them however much they hate me, I love them all.'

From what I could tell there was sadness in his eyes. I almost thought he was going to cry. 'You never knew about me.' He soothed. 'But you grew up under my watchful eye. You are more important than you ever think you are. Which is why…?'

'Just do it!' I snapped. 'I'll turn my back, and you do it.'

He nodded slowly. 'Okay!'

Hands shaking, I lit my cigarette and took a deep inhale and embraced the toxins into my body. With my back to the moonlight, I saw the shadow of his foot raised high above my head. I closed my eyes in anticipation of the pain of death.

There was a flash of light which burned my eyes through my eyelids. The crushing did not come. There was a crashing noise and a loud bang which shook the earth beneath my feet. Then I felt a hand upon my back. A soft friendly girl's voice said 'Amber, you have to come with me now.'

To be continued in this volume

Kate

I didn't write in part two, but if you have read it, my sister, Becky, bless her, has summed up my part pretty well. I had been very self-centred over the years, but I was coming to this realisation. I'd been working with the company nearly two years. I was with the company that Jess and Mandy were with briefly before that and Jimmy had worked there too. Yet still I didn't even know Jim well enough to know that his wife had died. Yet he knew all my shit. In his last moments that poor old man had been the friend to me that I had never been to anyone.

My emotions were everywhere. For a while, I'd lost my baby's father and my soul mate, but I'd got my sister back. Then John reappeared out of nowhere and fainted after screaming that he had just seen us die. I was relieved to have him back but confused as to where he'd been and what he was talking about. Then there was the pain of hearing Jim's tragic story and then the shock of him suddenly dying on us. All of this was going on while I was trying to keep my badly injured sister talking and trying not to give birth to my baby in the middle of a field.

I was squeezing John's hand as the pain got stronger, but he was barely aware of it. I was not prepared for what happened next and if you don't believe me, I won't blame you.

When I saw the lights coming, I honestly thought it was a search party who had come to help us. There were too many of them for me to give an accurate number. They had flame torches, and they were carrying weapons of all sorts including knives and possibly other things. It was like something out of the dark ages.

Before I had the chance to yell, 'Who the fuck are you?' They had grabbed me from all sides and had lifted me onto their shoulders. Yelling and screaming I tried to grab hold of John. He came alive from his fainting spell and tried to fight them off of me. He is a big tough bloke but there were too many of them, and I think they must have overpowered him, because soon there was no sign of him.

They were running with me on their shoulders and cheering like they were an ancient army on a battle charge. I will say to you now, for all my sharp-tongued tough woman attitude, I was crying like I did when I was a little girl, and I'd grazed my knees. I was scared, not only at the fact that I'd been kidnapped, but that these crazy people were going to drop me and hurt the baby.

Thankfully, the pace was steady, but they continued running, somehow avoiding the dykes and streams as though their route had been carefully planned. They must have been jogging with me on their shoulders for more than twenty minutes by the time we reached their destination. I had been facing backwards as they ran, looking for the light of the train, which I could no longer see, but as they spun me around, I saw a new light.

The brief sight I had of the light showed me that it came from a fire. As we would find out. These people were witches, so I'm not sure why they didn't just use magic to transport me. Maybe not all of them had the power to do what they did to Rob and Sharon and the others.

Around this massive fire, there were many people sitting back-to-back, shouting and screaming as though they were being held there. I tried to scream to them for help, but they were all so busy yelling for help themselves that my cries went unheard.

I was taken around the back of the fire to some sort of tent. It was dark colours and about the size of the small flat which John and I shared. The very thought of John made my heartburn. I lost him, then I got him back, but now he was gone again.

I was dropped down onto some sort of camp bed in the corner of the tent and felt something cold being pressed against the side of my head. I was about to scream once more when there was a click next to my head and a chilling voice, the kind which makes you sit up and listen for all your worth.

'Tell me your name,' It commanded as many of the masked people with torches either led out of the tent or stood back.

'Who are you people?' I cried, 'What do you want from me?'

There was no immediate answer, but the cold metal that rested against my head clicked. There was a bang that was so loud I almost gave birth there and then from the shock. With my ears and those around me ringing, the woman's cold and calm voice said, 'You will give me your full name and date of birth now, or the next bullet goes through your pretty little head.'

Obviously, she had sight problems or just hadn't seen me in the light. This is because when looks were handed out, I was so far back in the line that I gave up and went to the pub. That's actually quite a harsh thing to say when you consider that my sister and I are identical twins.

Sorry Becky love you

'Why the fuck are you pointing a gun at my head, you crazy bitch?' I yelled. The voice replied slowly. 'Full name, address and date of birth. Or I blow your brains out, and we cut the baby out of you.

'Alright!' I replied, with my heart pumping hard and more droplets of sweat forming on my face. The thoughts racing through my mind were not only 'Who are these people and why the hell are they pointing a gun at me? but what are they doing out here? What do they want with my baby and me, and why was my name so important?

My first thoughts were that I did not want my brains blown out. I wasn't quick thinking enough to give a false name, which would have been a better idea in hindsight.

'Kate... erm...' then I stopped 'No, that's not it.' I said out loud. People call me Kate for short, and they did it so often that even I almost forgot it wasn't my real name. As I waited for the next painful contraction to pass, then cleared my throat and started again.

'Katerina-Rose Maryanne Johnson.'

'And date of birth,' the woman replied in a calm voice. 'Sixteenth' I breathed, 'April 1978.'

'Can you confirm that this girl is who she says she is?' She asked a person who was obviously hidden from my sight. My thoughts suddenly changed to whoever it was hiding just outside the beam of light. There was a moment when I held my breath in anticipation of who it was that knew me. Was it a friend or was it a foe? Could this person have led these crazy gun-pointing, baby-snatching people to me?

'It's her,' said a voice that made my heart leap.

'John!' I screamed; I'd know his voice anywhere. How had he managed to fight them off and how had he got there so quickly? Why did he sound so calm and not breathless from running so fast to catch up? He was a big, tall, strong guy, and he was good at many things. We even had a bench press at home which he used a lot. Despite him being reasonably fit even I outpaced him when I wasn't heavily pregnant.

'John help me she's gonna kill me,' I yelled. There was a brief silence, but it was the woman who spoke first. 'I don't want to kill you.' She said calmly. 'But I had to threaten you to find out who you were.'

'But you didn't need to threaten me with a gun, you mad bitch,' I replied, adding that if she'd asked nicely, I would quite happily have told her.

'Oh, but I enjoy threatening people, it's fun,' she told me calmly with a hint of a laugh in her voice.

There was a sudden click of light which lit up the room momentarily and then a red glow and a puff of smoke.

I've already said that I'd spent time in rehab, so even if my kids are reading this, it won't be a surprise that I have smoked a lot of things in my late teens and very early twenties before I got clean. This smoke, however, was nothing like anything I have ever smoked.

The smoke seemed to be coming from a pipe in the hand of the lady with the gun. The smoke smelt sweet and sickly like the candyfloss they sold at the pleasure beach, which probably tastes good to some people but personally it makes me want to vomit.

'Get away from me with that foul-smelling shit' I shrieked.

'Who would have thought a former smoker and druggy would judge others.' She leered at me, blowing the smoke in my face, so I coughed.

'I'm not the kind of person to judge anyone, but just get that weird shit away from my baby and I and tell me why you've kidnapped us and why you're doing this.

'I require a new-born baby, and you my dear are going to give me yours, and you will not be leaving this tent alive.'

'Don't worry, Kate, sweetheart. I'll get us out of this.' John called from the other side of the tent in the dark.

'He isn't going to get you out,' she said in a matter-of-fact tone. 'We've stuck him in a chair and kept him alive so that we can shoot him if you try to get away, so don't even think about running.'

'Why do you want our baby?' I cried as more sweat ran down my face joining the tears that would not stop rolling out of my eyes.

She didn't answer for a minute and then she breathed deeply, and said, 'Okay, I suppose telling you the story while you give birth won't make any difference, seen as you're going to die tonight. Although,' she said after a pause, 'I have noticed that in the movies, the evil genius always feels the need to explain the plan to the victims.

Then they always seem to find some way of escaping.'

I had to agree with her there. John and I were both fans of James Bond and he

always escaped the trap after the bad guy revealed his plans.

The woman gave a small laugh. 'That's why I'm chaining you down.' To my shock, out of nowhere, I felt heavy chains around my arms and legs, and I was forced back onto the bed. As another chain looped around my neck and forced me backwards on the bed, the tent filled with light.

'How in the fuck did you do that?' I panted, speaking just in time to avoid being cut off by the strongest contraction I'd had so far.

'I'm Lord Voldemort,' The woman said with a hint of sarcasm. 'Don't you mean lady Voldemort? But that doesn't explain what you just did,' John shouted from his seat.

'Seriously, you don't know who Lord Voldemort is?' she said, glaring at him as he shrugged and added, 'Well you just said it was you, so we believed you.'

She looked at me, and back at John asking 'Seriously has neither of you read the Harry Potter books? 'Never heard of it,' We both said together. You have to remember that the first Harry Potter book had only been out for Three years at that point and was considered a children's book. However, I have since read it to all my kids and have

watched the movies.

'Basically, it's magic, and I'm the bad guy.'

'You don't say,' I snapped back at her. 'So, why me? Why my baby?'

'Well, let me tell you a story while we wait for the little one.

THE WITCH'S

HISTORY EXPLAINED.

CONTINUED BY KATE.

What the woman told me as I lie there, contracting, was her version of the past.

She told me that the Old Testament of the Bible had it all wrong. I knew that anyway because how exactly could God create the world in seven days when without the sun there was no such thing as day and night?

In her words, she told me that the earth and all of reality was created by evolution as I suspected it was, but that supposed evolution was controlled by the spirit who created the earth, and that spirit was not the one we call God.

Among her powers seemed to be this really horrifying ability to know things about me and my past and use them as examples to compare her story.

She started with a mention of when I had first been paired with John at work. In his first week he had made several sales, but I had told him not to sign them until I checked them for him. I had then taken half of his forms and copied out the names and addresses on them, passed them off as my own sales and destroyed the evidence. This was something I often did with new people because I was a bitch.

However, I had a conscience and a heart, and at the end of his first week I confessed to Mandy who went mad at what I'd done, and she had given me a stern warning and docked my next week's wages by the amount owed and paid it to John, claiming it was her mistake.

So, the woman knew this about me, and she used it as her example saying. 'The spirit you call God did not create the earth, he stole it from its true creator, and he took credit.'

'Ever since man has walked the earth, man has seemed to destroy nature. Using up natural resources, tearing down forests and enslaving the animals that once ran free on the planet in peace.'

'As God took control, the creator watched on in horror as his masterpiece was ruined by the human scum. He came up with a new plan to take back his world. He made his own beasts to destroy the human plague. A human-like race, human on the outside but with the ability to harness energy from the earth and use it to do magic. Their job was to use the powers sent to them to wipe out the human race and start the world all over again.'

'Alright, say I believe you just for a minute, which I don't,' I told her quite bluntly. 'If this is all true then why are us humans still here?'

She looked at me angrily for a second before continuing.

'Your god made his own army to defeat us.' She snapped 'For many years the two sides battled each other until finally the last two defenders of the earth were found hiding away. They were killed on this very night in 1590.'

'So, if this bullshit is correct, why, didn't the world end then?' I heard John shout from across the tent.

'Never mind that.' The woman retorted 'Let's just say that my people found ourselves no longer able to use our powers to directly kill the humans. The last two of the defenders gave their lives to spread the power from their bodies around the world. It protects the humans still to this day.'

'So, basically, you lot lost, and you're angry?'

'Angry no, greatly agitated.' She grinned 'Lost the battle, but not the war. In recent years, we have refocused

on making the humans fight themselves. The first and Second World Wars, among other things, were all my doing. It doesn't matter which side wins, as long as lots of people die. We planted the ideas and desires to kill each other into the heads of humans; we have people everywhere, in governments and terrorist organisations causing misery and destruction in every country in the world.'

'So why do you want our baby?' I screamed impatiently, breathing hard as the contraction passed.

'To speed things up a little' she smiled, looking around the tent and laughing.

On the night that the blood moon falls on the winter solstice, we have come to this place of great power to invoke the spirit of the great creator, by sacrificing a pair of virgins. When the spirit is summoned, we shall implant them in the newborn child, and we will break the spell that binds us from using our powers to kill.

'And then what?' I asked bravely. She went silent and then turned and looked at everyone in the room through the darkness.

'I don't understand the question.' She answered, and it was John who repeated my question to her. 'What do you do when the earth is wiped clear of mankind?'

'Well, we will cross that bridge when we come to it.' She told us hesitantly.

'Why use our baby, not somebody else's?' I demanded. 'I could go into some twisted story about how you and your twin are descendants of my greatest enemy, and your boyfriend here is one of us who has been convinced that he is a human.'

My heart stopped and my life as I knew it had ended. 'John, is this true?' I screamed, to which he replied, 'No, Kate. I don't know about any of this. I love you.' He cried.

'He's not lying,' she laughed horribly. 'He is so much under our control that he really believes what he's saying, but he truly is one of us. If he wasn't, how else do you think he got here to rescue you without being killed by one of one hundred thousand of my followers as they did to poor old Sue?'

'Let me ask you a question,' she grinned as my mind swerved from here to there to everywhere.

'You're living in his house and having his baby, but have you ever met any of his family?'

'He's Irish and they live in Belfast,' I screamed. 'It's been too far to visit them, or for them to visit us.' 'Don't listen to her Kate' John shouted.

'Or maybe it's because he's not really Irish and he is, as I say, one of us who has had his mind altered to believe he is human so that he can be believable enough to make a stupid human like you have a baby with him at the perfect time.'

'Alright so say we believe you,' John shouted out of the darkness. 'If Kate, who I really do love with all my heart is descended from your enemy who I'm guessing was a wizard or witch, why can she not do magic.'

The woman looked at me and smiled as though we were friends and whispered, 'She's a half-breed of several generations. Basically, somewhere along the line, one of the defenders of the earth mated with a human, creating a half-wizard from whom she is descended. She has only the tiniest hint of power in her as does her sister, but they had to do.'

'And what about me?' He asked, 'If I am really one, how come I can't do magic?'

Suddenly, the tent filled with light once more and I saw John strapped down to a chair with guns pointed at him in every direction.

'How did you survive that train crash, Johnny boy?' She smirked.

'What are you talking about?' He pleaded.

'You went back to get your friend, Jim, and you were on the train when it exploded, and your friends found your body, but were too terrified to tell your girlfriend in case she lost the baby, but here you are alive.'

Something crossed my mind suddenly. I remembered that when John found us, before fainting, he had told me to my face that he had just watched me die.

'John,' I yelled. There was silence as I asked quietly. 'Did you see me die?'

He shook his head. 'No,' He said breathing hard and sweating with nerves. 'I remember waking up on the other side of the train. Then I saw you, and Becky sat there with two other men. One of them looked like…'

'Kate I'm coming for you,' came another cry from the door of the tent. A man burst in, and all eyes fell on him.

Had my eyes failed me? There stood my boyfriend, John, panting and sweating. But if John was there who was in the chair?

'Oh, erm… yeah, we may have accidentally bumped two dimensions into each other.' The redheaded woman laughed.

'All here together,' She grinned 'Do you want proof that I brainwashed John here into having a baby with you. We only chose you as the host because your much healthier, non-smoking, non-drug-snorting sister has no interest in males.'

That was news to me. Although my sister was out and proud and though I hadn't discussed it at length, I was quite sure that she was bisexual and just happened to be dating a girl. That didn't mean she didn't like men. I've since been proved right about that but that's for her to talk about. Moving on…

'So, let me get this straight,' I breathed, resisting the desire to push once more. 'You arranged my whole life and my relationship?'

'We got you to clean up your act and make your body well enough to carry a child and arranged for the train to crash when and where it did.' She grinned as though we were having a friendly conversation.

'Of course, we could not have done it without our informant among your group. The one who for the past year and a half has been feeding us information on the promise that he was going to be made young again, like me, cure his cancer and bring back his dead wife.'

Another beam of light appeared out of nowhere, shining on the far corner of the tent where a young man sat in a chair, looking at the floor.

'I promised to make him young again and bring back his dead wife in return for making sure you'd be on that train on this marsh tonight.' She smirked, 'But I didn't promise not to put him back to his old self once I had you.'

She pointed a finger at the young man and light shot from it, and his hair turned grey, and his skin withered and wrinkled into a face I knew all too well.

'Jimmy!' I cried, hearing both versions of John do the same.

'How could you Jim?' I screamed. 'How could you do this?'

'I'm sorry,' he cried, 'She told me she would harm you all if I didn't do it!'

'And she's not harming us now?' John roared.

'Oh dear,' the redheaded woman smiled. 'Two more things before I go.'

'One, she...' teased pointing. 'I didn't really need you to push the baby out.'

With one swish of her finger, she had cut me open. Bits of my tummy were falling everywhere as she and I were screaming. Tears of anger and fear spluttered from my eyes. I screamed and struggled, but the chains pulled me down to the bed.

'You never met John's parents, did you, sweetie?' She mocked, holding my baby son just out of my reach.

'No give him back' I screamed, still not sure why I wasn't dead, with all my guts hanging out of me.

'Nice to meet you daughter-in-law.' She mocked waving and told me. 'I'll see you in hell very soon by the looks of that bleeding.'

'Oh, and the other thing,' She smiled as she headed for the exit, leaving me with blood pouring out of me. 'Just to prove this man is my son and one of us.' She clicked her fingers, and every one of the five or six guns that were pointed at the Johns and Jimmy's wentL off in their faces.

Charlie

Last time when I wrote a piece for volume two, I was stuck in Northern Ireland where Sammy and her family were very kind, letting me stay in her home. I still have nightmares about the time that she tried to bite me and drink my blood. Even though that was not our Sammy.

Since having to stay away from my family that night, I decided that I didn't want that to happen again. A lot of dads, especially, seem to want to spend time away from their families by going out to the pub after work and getting drunk with their mates. For me though, there is no point to having a family unless you're willing to spend time with them. For that, you have to make sacrifices, and after having had to spend that night away, I decided that my well-paid job, which involved lots of day trips to other countries, had to go.

My wife and I are lucky enough to be in a financial position in which I could quit my job and start up my own business from home. So, I am spending more time with my fantastic wife, and the kids. Especially as we were forced to have our kids much later in life than planned for health reasons.

When I left you last, I had just been attacked by Sammy the vampire, and then I was saved by Jenny, the vampire slayer.

I wasn't sure how hard I had bumped my head. Vampires and witches, seriously?! I have heard of some very fucked up people drinking blood and people who follow Wicca as their religion. However, I was pretty sure that Wiccans could not fly and that sick people who drink the blood of others are all locked up in institutions.

This girl had just flown in from nowhere and helped me to kill a vampire, and now I was on her back, flying high above the marshes searching for the people who had got off of the train.

The first strange thing I noticed—other than the fact that I was flying several metres above the earth on the back of a teenage girl I'd only just met—when we crossed over the railway tracks, there was no sign of the road. I must have been disoriented because it seemed like we were heading into the marshes on my right-hand side, even though we had gone left.

Also, if we had turned left, the fire from the train would have been behind us to our left, but it was clearly ahead of us to our right.

'The world must seem pretty crazy to you right now,' Jenny called into my ear, as I clung to her for dear life with my heart pounding and senses like you get on a roller coaster as it rushes along the tracks. Although now there was no track that I could see holding us up.

It was the scene from the Snowman, where the snowman and the boy are walking in the air to the voice of Peter Auty—not Aled Jones, as people think it is.

'Crazy?' I yelled. 'People are disappearing. Sammy turned into a vampire and tried to kill me. You can fly, and I'm flying on your back. That's not crazy,' I added with a hint of sarcasm. 'Just a normal day at the office for me.'

'You don't work in an office. You're a door-to-door salesman,' came her blunt reply. 'Obviously, you don't understand sarcasm.' She replied that it was no time to be making jokes.

'You see what's wrong down there?' she yelled,

'There's plenty wrong everywhere right now,' I retorted.

'True.' she shouted over the wind, 'But down there is totally fucked up, and there's no getting out of here unless we can fix this.'

She explained as she hovered over the marsh, trying to pick people out. 'Some very powerful and evil people have done a bad thing. A spell seems to have backfired, causing alternate worlds to crash into each other, leaving an invisible border between worlds on the line of the railway.'

'What does it all mean?' I stuttered.

'It means…' she sniffed. 'Two worlds, two trains, several people now missing and eight groups of people looking for help. The four groups that went along the tracks, two are heading for dead ends where they will have to go a lot further than expected for help, and two of them will find each other. As for the other four groups and the missing people…'

She stopped and turned and pointed to something. From up in the sky, it looked like lava flowing, but instead, there were a large number of people with lights moving quickly. 'There's enough of them to fill Wembley Stadium, and look.'

She turned us around and crossed over the tracks to show a similar scene. 'Whichever way they go, your friends are walking straight into the fires of Hell, and we need to warn them.'

'Who are these people and what are they doing out here?'

'Let's not worry about what they're doing right now,' She sniffed heavily 'Let's just get down there and…' She paused and shuddered to say, 'Not now, no, no, not now, please.'

Before I could ask, she took a rattling breath and there was a big, 'Ah, ah, ah, aaacchhhooo'

Let me tell you something, if ever you find yourself flying on the back of a witch over two hundred metres in the air, try to pick one that doesn't have a cold, because one sneeze up there can be fatal.

The sneeze flung me over Jennie's shoulders and off into the sky where I began to fall.

I was spinning ever closer to the ground, and my life was starting to flash in front of me. Starting with the moment I was born, I saw my mother, young and healthy and smiling. Then I saw her again with her young body only twenty-five years old, riddled with cancer as she spoke her last words to her five-year-old son.

'Charlie, life is a gift you need to use well.' Then it was my mum's funeral, where I'd never known such sadness and my dad was drinking heavily.

The first time I met Dave and his cute little sister, then nights out in the pub with Sarah, Dave and his cute little sister. (Among others)

Then Dave's and Sarah's joint funeral where there was a parade scooters and motorcycles. I had spent the whole service holding the hand of his cute little sister, Then my father's funeral where I also held hands with Dave's cute little sister, as well as my fiancée who didn't take it too well. That's probably why the next memory was of her giving me the ring back and telling me to give it to the right person. Then there was the train crashing, and the next thing was me kissing Dave's little sister about twenty minutes earlier.

So, you'd be guessing that with the last memory being only twenty minutes ago it would be time for me to hit the ground. I remembered in the scouts where we sang a Second World War song where an RAF man's parachute fails him, and it tells of his thoughts before he dies a horrible death. Google it. The USA version is called blood on the risers. I closed my eyes and began to sing 'Gory, gory, what a hell of a way to die' Over and over.

That is until a voice shouted, 'Hey, what are you singing that for? You're not gonna die while I'm here to save you.'

I opened my eyes to see the ground below my head as I hung in the air only inches from the grass. In the light of my head torch, I could see the girl, Jenny, standing a few feet away with a relieved smile on her face and her finger pointed at me. She was somehow causing me to levitate above the ground. She casually twisted her fingers as though to turn me the right way up.

'You left that a bit close!' I said sharply as I fell to the floor with my knees quivering.

'Oh, well, thank you for saving me,' she said to herself in a sarcastic tone, replying, 'Oh no problem at all just don't go randomly falling out of the sky again.'

'But you were the one who dropped me.' I protested, to which she replied, 'I did nothing of the sort. In fact, we haven't even met before.'

'So, you and I didn't just fight a vampire and kill it, then fly off into the sky?'

'No, I've no idea what you're talking about.' She reiterated.

'But you just dropped me out of the sky.'

'I did not.' She repeated, 'I was helping your colleague. I heard you falling and came to your aid, and without me, you'd be dead.'

'So, you're not Jenny or Buffy the Vampire Slayer who just saved my life and then dropped me, but you are a Jenny, and you look like the one who dropped me, and you're magic like the one that dropped me.'

'It wasn't me,' She says, smiling, 'but I think I know what's happened.'

In a shot, she had grabbed me, and we were airborne again. This time she flew at a speed that nearly made my stomach come out of my bottom.

My head was spinning by the time we stopped, and I could hear somebody swearing loudly and saying, 'Shit, I killed him.'

'Have you lost something, Jenny?' Jenny said to herself. I say to herself, because Jenny, who had her arms tightly around me was suspended around a hundred metres above the earth and talking to Jenny, who was the spitting image of her who was looking down and swearing and crying.

'I dropped a guy who I was trying to save, and he's dead.' She said sadly.

'I thought we were staying hidden from the humans, not taking them flying,' the jenny who had me on her back retorted with a wink as though she was teasing. Acting all casual as I clung to her for dear life.

'Well, he was being attacked by a vampire.' She protested

'Well, luckily for you, he's right here.'

As if being in the air was not scary enough, my heart went up beyond my mouth into my head when one strange flying vampire slaying witch girl threw me several feet into the dark towards the other who this time caught me easily and apologised.

'Sorry I dropped you, Charlie.' She said rather earnestly.

'Apology excepted as long as you don't do it again.' I breathed, my heart racing harder than a horse in the Grand National.

'Let me introduce you to myself,' she said with a smile. Well, I assume she was smiling, because her head was away from me, but there was a hint of a laugh in her voice.

'We've already met, remember? When we fought the vampire and then you dropped me.' I reminded her.

'Of cause' Was her reply. 'You met me, but now you've met the other me.'

The other flying girl was now right up beside us and looking from one to the other in the light, I could see that the pair of them were identical.

'No, not twins,' they said, speaking so perfectly in sync with each other. 'We can read your mind, and we know what you're thinking. We are two incarnations of the same person from parallel worlds.'

'What there's... there's two of you?' I stuttered. 'How the fuck is that possible?'

The other Jenny looked at me with a weird expression and said calmly. 'So, you've just found out that there are witches, vampires, werewolves and trolls. Yet the hardest thing of all to believe is that there are two of us?'

'There are trolls too?' I yelled, to which she replied, 'Yep, but there's no time to explain everything. We need to get these people who are scattered all over the place back into one place, while we figure out what to do about putting the world back together.'

'We need a plan and quick,' The Jenny who had me on her back told us, urgently pointing towards the ever-growing lights gathering in the distance on either side.

'I found the virgin, Amber Spelman. She was taken by a troll, apparently. He told her what was going on and she asked him to kill her so she couldn't be used. I sort of rescued her from him and fucked things up again.'

So, in the confusion of everything, the fact that Amber had tried to have herself killed kind of went over my head.

The Jennies quickly came up with a plan.

They planned that my Jenny and I would seek out all the survivors and search parties and point them back in the direction of the trains and tell them to hide themselves. The other Jenny would go to the train and try to use her powers to heal the wounded and then she would go to somewhere that she called the village of Freaks. Both were in agreement that they would no longer try to hide their powers.

So, what happened next was we flew north, and that was where we found Chris, Rachael, Ben and Carol. Who, as you know, were shocked to see us as we showed them the way back? We went up and down the marsh, from end to end, looking for people to tell to return. However, unfortunately many of them had already been captured. Including a group clearly including myself—the other me.

Mandy, Sadie, and Sammy seemed not to have been caught, but neither could we find them. The only one of the missing people we saw was James walking with a load of men in masks.

After a long while, we spotted a girl on her own, wandering in the field at the side of the tracks, way up past the second train.

'I know who this one is,' Jenny whispered. 'Seen as she's alone, I will see if I can get you both on my back.' As she set me down, I called gently, 'Jessie, sweetheart, are you okay? It's me, Charlie.' The girl turned as I walked towards her. As the light hit her, she smiled. This was Jessie, but it was not the one I left. This Jessie still had her glasses intact and the look on her face turned from a smile into a sort of scowl.'

'Oh, you.,' She spat, Suddenly, there was a scream from behind me, and I spun around to see Jenny being held in a headlock by a big dark figure.

'Helping humans are we girl?' Came a thundering voice from her attacker. 'Well, if you want to help them so much, maybe you can die with them.'

I made a grab to try and help Jenny, but whoever or whatever had her was red hot and burned my hands.

'Charlie!' Jenny yelled as though she was in considerable pain. 'Take this Jess and do what you can to keep each other safe while I deal with this.'

The massive dark figure spoke to us in a roar. 'I'll be back for you once this one is in chains.'

All of a sudden, Jenny wriggled out of the headlock and shot into the sky, shouting. 'You'll have to catch me first.'

The other Jessie stood there with her hand on her chest staring up at the sky, saying breathlessly. 'What the hell is going on? Who the fuck were they? And give me a fag now?'

I looked at her in disbelief. Where I came from, Jessie hated smoking and couldn't smoke anyway because of her asthma, and despite having been engaged to a very heavy smoker, I'd never smoked myself seeing as both my parents died from cancer. I looked her up and down for a moment, not sure how to tell her I didn't have any cigarettes to offer.

However, she looked at me as though I had insulted her, before saying rudely. 'I asked for a fag more than thirty seconds ago, so I expected to be smoking by now. You are the most useless person I have working for me and the last person I would want to have saving me, you snivelling little weasel.'

Just when I thought this night could not get any more fucked up, The Jessie I had known since childhood was and is the loveliest, kindest, smartest, hardworking person I have ever had the pleasure to know. Trust me to get landed with looking after her evil twin.

Rachael

So, we were walking back to the tracks in a shivering silence and doing exactly what the woman who came from the sky told us to do. Nobody spoke about it. I think we all thought the cold was driving us insane. I was icy cold, having fallen into mud as I explained in volume two. I clung to Ben, telling myself that I needed to make a point of thanking his girlfriend for lending him to me.

Before joining J&M, I was a secondary school teacher, and I've since worked as a teacher again for many years. I teach geography and history, but I'm sure even my colleagues in the science department couldn't explain how a woman had just shot a line of light out of her finger to light the way back to the tracks.

The light was the strangest thing I had ever seen, apart from a person flying on the back of another person. It could all be a hallucination because I was so deathly cold, despite Ben's efforts. The beam of light seemed to be something only the four of us, Chris, Carol, Ben and I could see. The light was always at the centre of the group, keeping us together, and if we had to go around something, the light would move with us to compensate. When I looked behind us, the light where we had been had vanished.

The time on my watch as we finally reached the debris of the train read 1:20 a.m. I never checked the time when we started walking, but it was now more than three hours and twenty minutes since the train left the station. It couldn't have been that long between the train leaving the station and coming off of the rails. Who knows how long we were being organised into groups? I was shocked to see that none of the other search parties had returned.

We stayed hidden from the train from and from sight, as we were told to do by the flying lady. We laid in the grass on the same side of the tracks. I would have ignored the instructions to stay hidden and gone to help the injured in whatever way I could, but the decision to stay was made as a group.

We saw the lights coming toward the train from the far side of the marsh, thinking that it must be some sort of help come at long last. We could have gone to meet them, but we were all too scared of what we'd seen to move from our hiding place until we knew they were friendly.

The lights came and went away again as quickly as they had come. I wanted to break ranks and run to the train to see what had just happened. Ben and Chris, however, pulled me back saying in hushed voices. 'Look, there's somebody coming up the tracks.'

I looked to my right and to my left, then I ducked back down in the grass. There were lights coming from my lefthand side. I counted four of them walking fast towards us.

I looked on as they came closer, keeping my mouth shut and staying out of sight. One thing that struck me is that there were four lights. All the groups that went down the tracks had three people. That must of meant that Jessie and her group had found one of the missing people.

'Or it could be somebody different altogether,' Chris said, adding in a small voice that if there were people who could fly, and people we should be scared of hanging around, it could be anyone.

As they came closer, I heard voices, but didn't see their faces because they made their way down towards the train. I heard their voices and it surprised me beyond belief. One of them was Jessie, and one of them was a man who I assumed was Charlie, but then it couldn't have been because we saw Charlie, so it must have been James. Then if we saw Charlie and James were there, then if they had lost a person and gained a person then there would be three, but there was four. Maybe the freaky witch woman dropped him back with them. What if they found two people?

It didn't matter, they were alive. Then suddenly I recognised the other voices. They could not possibly be there. Sadie and Mandy had gone the other way, yet there they were returning to the train with Jessie and Tom? Tom who lost his head.

Georgie

This is Katie lead author. Georgie wrote this a while back and was unable to send it to me. However, the book was delayed due to our lovely editor catching corona virus and Georgie returned to the UK believing this would be her first of three contributions to volume four. This is why Amber thinks Georgie didn't take part.

I want to start by saying that I wrote this piece a while back. But I didn't foresee myself being in a situation where I couldn't email it to Katie. I'm back in the Uk at the moment but at the time I was many miles away doing what it is that I do. I don't like to talk about what I do because I hate blowing my own trumpet it makes a horrible noise and I don't want to. Other people can talk about what I do if they like. I suppose if that's what they want.

Basically, I was in a foreign country, helping with a project to help the locals. I was mucking in and getting my hands dirty. I was doing things that a double amputee in her forties possibly should not have attempted, and I slipped. There was a crack and a bang, and I broke my left arm and damaged both my prosthetics. I didn't tell anyone what had happened at the time, partly because I didn't want to worry my friends and partly because I was so far from any big civilization that there was no internet and no phones.

Life has been a challenge, but I do love challenges and the harder I make it for myself, the more ex-citing it is to come out of it alive.

Basically, right now, after years of freedom, I'm confined to my wheelchair while an insane amount of money is spent on new prosthetics to get me walking again. I'm bursting to talk about life now but if I do that before I talk about life back then it will have no context.

For a little recap, seeing as I don't know how long it will be since you read the first part of my story.

I'm the only surviving member of the Aricot family. I awoke from a coma in a hospital in the Swiss Alps in 1996. I lost both my legs and banged my head so hard that I couldn't remember anything about my life before-hand. My family, including my gorgeous twin sister Maggy Grace, my younger brother, and both parents, were killed. Driving my dad's Aston Martin to our family's hideout in the Alps, I hit my dad's other car from behind and knocked it down a mountainside before plunging down it after them.

We don't need to go over this again other than to say that I was a crazy legless hermit who behaved like Lieutenant Dan from forest Gump and didn't care if I lived or died for a while before I met Jessie and Mandy, and they saved me.

That night after the train blew up, and I thought I saw Amber snatched by a monster. I banged my head and woke up in a first aid tent with the lovely young nurse Katie and another girl. I had thought it was all a dream. Katie was under the impression that the other young woman and I were sisters, but that was impossible. But as you read in volume two, seemingly there is more to heaven and earth than we could ever possibly know. When the woman awoke, she knew me, and she had the same photographs in her wallet that I had with both of us and our parents and our little brother.

She even had the other half heart necklace which I still wear to this day. The necklace was specially customised so it would only fit one other peace and that was buried in with Maggy Grace in the family burial plot. (Yes, rich posh families still have family burial plots but I'm not going there when I die.)

I'd always hated myself for being the driver who killed my family.

Of course, people will say that being a bad driver doesn't make you a bad person. I wasn't drunk, and I wasn't speeding.

Believing it was all a dream, I played along with it, and I sat and drank Coco with Katie and this girl who looked like my dead sister. Maybe if other people hadn't confirmed that it wasn't a dream, I might still have thought the whole thing was.

Then again, the coco was too delicious to be a dream, and I don't know about you, but I don't recall sneezing in my dreams unless there's some sneezing-based theme to the storyline of the dream. That never happens.

Unless it's still 1999 and I'm fast asleep on the train having a dream that spanned over two decades, then we have to conclude it was real. How we both came to be there, I don't know. The other woman was convinced that I was her bad dream and that she would wake up. Yet after her initial yelling and screaming at me to stop haunting her. She calmed down and talked to me. Katie must have still thought we both had amnesia because she wasn't buying the fact that we could not be sisters.

Well, if you remember from part two the other woman who seemed to be my sister claimed that she had a life similar to the one I had. She worked for a sales company called Jessica's enterprises, (Not

Jessica and Mandy's enterprises which I worked for) She didn't get the chance to say how it was that she got to be out there in the middle of the field. She hadn't been chasing a monster that had her friend like I had been. I think we were going to get on to that. The thing that stuck with me, though, was her claim that we had switched identities. I had a brain injury, and I woke up remembering nothing. If she was telling the truth and we had switched passports, I would not have known. But then did things in other worlds have other ways of working? Who knows? I was more interested in learning to live with my disabilities and the fact that I killed my family. We were identical twins, so not even the surrounding people would know I was not who I thought I was.

Jennies' words rang out in my ears again as though etched on my brain. 'The key to your survival is Amber.' Well, that was not an amber coloured key. It was Amber, the person who, in the space of a few minutes, turned from what we all thought was a grumpy, rude, self-obsessed hormonal teenager into.... Well, a brave young woman who risked her life to save mine, so whatever she does in life from now on she is wonder woman to me. Before I come off track it was Jennies next words that made sense. 'When worlds collide, you will meet your Grace.'

This girl who looked like my sister said she was from a world like ours but there were differences like her being alive and me being dead. What if somehow worlds had collided? (I'm guessing that you know from other peoples accounts of the evening that a collision of worlds was what happened, but I didn't know that at the time.) So, I now somewhat impossibly had met my twin Maggy Grace, but again she said she was me and I was her. That left only one possibility, and that was this. I was not who I thought I was.

It explained so much. When I located my family's stuff, I found identical diaries. We kept diaries in the days when we didn't all have our own laptops and smart phones and social media. I kept them with photographs and the few things I wanted before I let our many family homes to tenants or sold them. One family shouldn't have more that one home. Being on my own I didn't need a house or my own staff. (I didn't sack them they were given other jobs in my farther's company)

So, I kept all the diaries, but I read only mine, never hers. Maggy Grace's private thoughts were hers and not for me to read, even in the event of her death. But I read my diary over and over. I just could not connect with the person who wrote the words. She was nice enough, but some of the things she moaned about in writing did my head in. I couldn't find a connection between myself and the whining spoilt brat who had rich girl problems like parties dresses and not getting the sports car she wanted for our 17th birthday. She wasn't a bad person, and she loved being a twin. She worshiped her sister and brother, but she wasn't me in any shape or form.

But that was Mary Georgie's diary. I didn't connect with her because I was Maggy Grace the sister she adored and looked up to even though we were equals. I'd been reading the wrong girls diary the whole time. So I did meet my Grace… when worlds collided just as the spirits told Jenny. But it was not this girl. For the first time since waking up from my coma, I met myself.

This is about where we left part two. There was no time to dwell on what she told me. There was a rush of people coming into the tent shouting about being attacked.

It didn't hit me at first what I was seeing. This group of people burst in in a panic. They were carrying a person with them. There was blood everywhere coming from an injury to a man who they carried. They put him down on the bed where I'd been when I woke up.

Katie went to take one look at him and went white as a sheet. She looked from the man on the bed to me and to my possible sister and to the others. They expected her to do something, but she froze like a statue. I could see the panic in her face and so could everyone. Even though I was concussed myself I could see the youth in her face. There was no way this woman was a calm experienced nurse who knew what she was doing. I saw an injury on the man's leg pouring blood. An arterial bleed. If somebody didn't do something he would bleed out.

The people who brought him in were clueless as to how to help him, but I had an idea that might b of some help. Any help I could give was better than nothing.

I fumbled to remove my clothing to soak up the blood. I threw down my coat and ripped off my blouse. My voice, usually slow and small, was loud and commanding as I told a stander by to wrap them around his leg. One around the bleed and another above.

'More clothes around the gash to soak the blood.' I told them. As I removed the only thing, I had capable of tying a tight knot to stop the blood from above the wound. (My Bra)

I tied the bra as tight as I could around the top of his leg as the others held him down, putting pressure on in to stop the bleed. Finally, breathlessly, I managed to tie it off, stopping the bleed temporarily. In the unlikely event that we could get help out here there could still be a slim chance of him living. Remember, our phones didn't work and there was no such thing as the air ambulance to save us in those days.

I sat there on the grass in the light of the gas lamp breathing deeply. I didn't stop to wonder where in my life I gained the knowledge to save a man's life like that despite my own disabilities. The girl who we believed to be my sister was smiling at me with pride for my efforts. While everyone else looked from me to Katie who was in tears.

Poor Katie looked around everyone. Her face filled with shame as she screamed.

'I'm sorry I'm not a nurse, I'm a Kid. I was at school yesterday! Mum told me to put her uniform on.'

'It's okay,' A few people murmured, while others tutted a bit.

More of them were staring at me now. It was natural, as they didn't know who I was or how I came to be there. However, they were not staring at my legs. They were looking further up.

My wig had fallen from me in the panic. Not even some of my close friends knew I was bald. Well, that's just it, really. I wasn't, but much of my scalp was damaged, and I couldn't grow hair in some parts of my head. I shaved the parts I could and wore my wig over the top.

'Have you guys never seen a skin head woman with no legs before?' I asked quietly. No body spoke.

Katie raised her hand slowly before speaking and she was pointing down at my topless body and said nervously. In the confusion, I had totally forgotten I was naked.

'Given that most of these are men and you're naked, I think they're looking at your tit's.' She smiled, before adding nervously in a whisper. 'I know I was. You have a nice pair.'

'Thanks, I think.' I smiled in return, a little put out.

The girl who claimed she was my sister or me which ever it was kindly handing me her coat to cover myself up. A smile beaming across her face. 'There you are, Doctor Margaret Grace; I knew you were in there.'

'Doctor?' I questioned, 'I've never been a doctor. I don't even know what I did to save him. I'm a saleswoman and before that I was a rich snobby brat.'

'Well,' she told me frowning as others looked on. 'You were never a rich snobby brat. That was me. You might not have got to do it because of the accident in your world and your death in mine, but I'm telling you. Rich spoilt billionaire or not. After you took a year out you were going off to university to study to be a doctor.'

I didn't have time to process this new information. There was a grunt from the man in the bed who I had just saved. He began to have some sort of seizure. He shook the bed and hissed and rattled. He began to turn red, and hair seemed to be growing out of him.

'Fuck me what happened to this man?' Katie bellowed, taking over. 'What caused that cut on his leg to be so bad?'

They all looked around at each other, shrugging. 'We were being chased by this crowd of violent people with weapons. We didn't see what got him, but there were these big terrifying creatures. They seemed to run out into the marshes, and we escaped. 'What sort of creatures were they?' She demanded. But her question did not need to be answered.

More hair was growing out of all areas. His hands were changing, claws were growing out of them. Teeth were bursting out of his mouth.

A lone voice from the back answered. 'Wolves'

Sadie 2

Unfortunately, life has those moments where everything changes. A little over ten minutes ago I was with my friends walking as fast as my lungs would let me to try to help look for the missing people. Now, however, only moments later, I was locked in a cage, thrashing to get out and go after the people I had been trying to help.

I'm quite sure that you will not have started reading this book without reading volumes one and two. You'd be a bit of a twit if you hadn't, so I will just give you a brief reminder. Just after Sammy found a dying girl that she thought was herself, I was snatched away by a huge dog, which ripped me to shreds. Then just as my life finished flashing before me, the choir of angels were singing, and I was spouting my own wings when suddenly I was brought back from the dead. It appeared I had been saved by

some sort of weird bloodsucking people. Or for a better word, vampires.

I had gone from a mild-tempered young woman into a raging beast in a matter of moments. I didn't know right then and there what I had become. I only knew that I wanted blood and meat in my mouth right now and it didn't matter how I got it.

There were people standing around the cage shouting and swearing over my growling. They were first in line to be eaten if I could only get out of the cage. I seemed to have gained some sort of superhuman strength, but even that was not good enough to break whatever this cage was made of.

Above my scratching and snarling, I heard a sudden cry to my right-hand side, which stopped me in my tracks. It was a child's voice—a terrified little girls scream. There was a child in the cage with me. 'Lunch time'

'No, Sadie, you can't eat a child,' I told myself, but I couldn't listen to myself, because the feeling was too strong.

I wasn't a human anymore, I was a big mad, vampire dog. In the movies, vampire dogs eat little girls for breakfast. Then again, I don't really remember seeing a movie with a vampire dog, so that's probably not accurate. Even Twilight—which would not be out for a few years yet doesn't have vampire dogs.

The child was about eight or nine years old, and from the small light there was in the tiny cage, I could see she had curly blonde hair like the child played by Kirsten Dunst in interview with a vampire—which I have seen since.

I no longer cared who I bit or why I was in a cage with a child, and I didn't care who she was or why she was there with me. I ravaged her with my hands or paws or whatever it was that was now on the end of my arms, and I opened my enormous mouth and bit down on the nearest part of her I could find. Then I heard myself yelp in pain.

It was the kind of yelp that my pet Labrador Freddy makes when I accidentally stand on his foot. My teeth had become strong as iron, but they had no effect on the girl and in fact, it hurt me badly to bite her.

'Don't be silly' I heard her say in a quiet voice. 'You can't bite me now any more than I can bite you again.'

I stood still glaring. 'Erm... What the hell?' I heard myself ask, although I wasn't sure if it was me because I had turned into a dog, and I didn't think dogs could talk. 'Like I said,' She replied softly, 'Whatever you are now you can't bite one of your own kind.'

'What do you mean my own kind?' I probed with an alarming snarl in my voice. 'Werewolves' she said simply 'You have been bitten by a werewolf, then the vampires sucked you dry, then they gave you their own blood so you didn't die and locked you in here with me because they didn't know how you would react.'

This was all too weird, and I needed a rational explanation of what was going on.

'Wait, I know what happened,' I said suddenly, after a moment's pause, 'After the train crashed Sammy gave me one of her cigarettes.'

'Well, I don't know Sammy, but smoking is very…' The girl started to say without moving her mouth, but I cut her off without moving my own. 'I know, smoking is bad for you.' I snapped adding that, unlike a lot of people, I am a selective smoker, and I only smoke if I'm offered, and often still decline them. 'She must have given me some of her strong wacky baccy without me realising, and I am just stoned and tripping, and when I wake up, I'm going to slap her,' I raged angrily.

'You need to come and explain it to her,' The girl called calmly to the figures outside of the cage, adding, 'She thinks they gave her drugs. But you owe her the honest truth.' I noted that this time she opened her mouth.

'Nobody gave you any drugs,' said a man coming out of the crowd. I jumped back, and found myself on all fours, and hungry for blood once more, until I saw the man's fangs. 'It's our fault this happened to you, and it would have been kinder to let you die,' he said in a gruff voice.

Something in me noted that the man opened his mouth to speak to me. 'If this isn't drugs then what is it?'

'He can't hear you when you don't open your mouth,' The little girl explained. I tried as hard as I could to speak from my mouth, rather than my head, but all that came out was a gruff bark. 'You can't talk like a human when you're a dog.' She added, 'Well, then, how in the fucking hell do I fucking talk to anyone?'

'Well,' she said with a snarl in her own voice, 'If you were able to use your mouth, I'd start with washing it out with soap, and apologise for using that filthy language, and I might consider translating for you.'

'I am sorry, imaginary girl,' I told her sarcastically.

'I'll ignore your sarcasm,' she added with a little smile, before using her mouth to speak to the man.

'Unsurprisingly, she thinks we are the by-product of smoking weed,' she told him, adding, 'But I think we need to explain who we are, why we're here, and what happened to her. Then you can explain how I got free.'

He looked at me slowly and reached into the cage to touch my side. it was surprisingly calm and comforting. 'You have heard folktales and myths of vampires and werewolves, I presume?'

'I don't like horror movies,' I told her. '...but I know about Dracula, because I visited Whitby Abbey with my boyfriend and I saw the Wolfman once, and that was enough.'

'She hates horror films, and her boyfriend is insanely boring, but I think she gets it,' the girl told him.

'You understand what this all means?' the girl asked with a sad look. 'No part of this is seeming right. I've just turned from a normal Twenty-four-year-old into a vicious dog.'

'You're not a dog, you're a werewolf, like I am, only, not like I am,' she corrected.

'You're a wolf too?' I asked, realising that I should not be surprised at this, seeing as she was also in the cage.

She nodded and looked away from me as though she was ashamed of something.

'Every time there's a full moon, this happens to me,' She smiled sadly. 'Every full moon since I was bitten, I've been taken out here to the marsh, to run free where the others are, where I can't harm people.'

'Okay, breathe,' I told myself. So, there are werewolves, and I'm one of them now, and they come out here, because they have a conscience and don't want to hurt people. Apparently, vampires existed too. So, a was a calm girl, and I took the news quite well really, I think.

'So, werewolves and vampires are friends then?' I quizzed her.

'She asked if we are friends,' She told the man in a hard tone, which she then softened as she asked him, 'I don't know. Are we friends?'

The man then turned to me rather than her and said, 'There are two types of vampire in this world, the few who have transformed and freely drink the blood of humans, and those like me, don't make a habit of drinking blood and use our strength to protect those fortunate enough not to have our problem. The werewolves like us can't help what they are, so we help them to get the exercise they need on a full moon, without letting them kill anyone.'

'We stay at the freaks camp out on the marsh one night before and after the full moon,' The young girl added, 'Then, before the full moon, the vampires spread out in a circle several miles wide, so that we can run and hunt cattle, but they can use their strength to stop us getting out into the community and killing humans.'

'And in answer to your question, young lady,' the man said turning to her with soft eyes, and says, 'Yes, we are friends, and we are sorry we let you go too far, but we were distracted not only by the train exploding, and the fresh human flesh on the bones of the survivors. One of our vampires went mad and bit one of the girls, and while we were dealing with that, we broke ranks and let you go, and I am sorry to both of you.'

'What does he mean, sorry to us both?' I asked the girl, still without moving my lips.

She looked at me sadly and had tears in her eyes, and said, 'You must know by now what the hunger for human flesh is like,' she said with a big sob.

'I don't know how these vampires keep themselves from drinking human blood. When I smelt human flesh and blood and saw there was nothing protecting it, I could not stop myself—no matter how hard I fought it— from biting and killing the first human I came into contact with.'

'You killed somebody?' I screamed as she turned her tearful face away. I was selfishly hoping upon hope that she was not going to say that she had killed one of my friends. However, she turned to the man who was still outside of the cage as I heard myself barking and snarling with anger.

'Tell her who I killed and what happens now.'

The man smiled at me uneasily, and said, 'We felt your fear as you lay dying, and felt that saving what we could of you even like this would give you some hope of continuing with the life you wanted to have.'

'What-what is he saying?' I asked the girl. I did know something of the mythology of vampires and wolves. Obviously, it seemed that I was now a wolf and that showed that my theory, the one I was scared of was probably right. If you survive the bite of a werewolf, then you become one and if you survive the bite of a vampire, you also become one.

If this was not some weird drug-induced dream, then I had seemingly been bitten by both a werewolf and several vampires that night.

I could feel a rage building up inside me. It was a feeling that calm placid little me had never felt before. I could see why they had saved me. I didn't want to live with the implications of what had happened. I remember my dying vision in which I bit my boyfriend Carl at our wedding. I couldn't let that happen, but I would rather have died than be put in a position where I had to break up with him and stay away from my friends and family for their own safety.

Why could those vampires not have just let me die? The rage was building inside but when I let out an angry yell all that came out of my mouth was a snarling roar as I smashed myself against the bars of the cage. All of a sudden anger overcame me, so much that blood was pulsing through my veins, causing my legs and body to be overcome with power. My strength was too much even for a cage made of silver.

I didn't just want blood and flesh, I wanted revenge on those who had saved me rather than let me die with dignity. I made short work of the cage and soon I was out into the night and ready for blood and revenge, and I didn't care if I killed friend or foe.

Jessica

So, in her piece written earlier this year, Katie told you that I was sat writing with her and Georgie (Who was skyping us from her home in Kenya) at a hotel in Cromer, which is owned by her brother-in-law and sister-in-law. Well, what really happened is that we tried to write, but Katie's lovely sister-in-law, Katarzyna, She's a lovely Czech girl—I say girl, but she's about thirty—who doesn't drink herself, offered us a lush bottle of wine, so it would be rude not to drink it. It was also rude not to drink the second bottle, which we paid for of course—you know what happens when the girls get together. We drank so much wine that we had to leave our cars in Cromer and get our husbands to pick us up.

The writing I did was quite awful, so I must admit I've had to start this section again.

So, book one started with twenty-three-year-old me and the rest of the team on the train and I had a horrible cold. In December of 2019, nearly twenty years to the day forty-three-year-old me is now sitting on the train with a cold.

This time is different though. I'm on one of the new trains on the Liverpool Street line with plug sockets Wi-Fi and comfy seats. I've been having cyber dinner with my husband and kids on zoom and decided to kill the next couple of hours.

So my husband and I had to have a conversation in 2016 after the Brexit vote and stupid mess of an election. He told me that if I stood as an independent Member of Parliament for East Norfolk I would win. I told him that independents never win. We decided to have a bet on it. I ran for parliament as an Independent in the 2019 election.

I don't know what the hell I did but I somehow lost the bet and got elected, and now guess what? I'm on the train on the way home from being inducted into the House of Commons.

Enough about that, I'm getting off track with talk of politics I'm supposed to be telling what happened that night, so let's move on.

Right now, I'm at the back of the train away from the other passenger slurping a huge cup of coffee, and I have another sneezy cold. I'm wondering if the bad people are causing my cold. I'm also hoping the kids are not being too much trouble for their dad, because I hate leaving them, but I couldn't drag them all to London. That would not be fair on them.

As an MP I will not be getting a second home near London as I don't want to move my kids and I want to stay in the community I serve with the people who elected me. So guess this what I'll make the trip to the big smoke to mingle with others control our country when I have to.

Jessica Reynolds of course is not my real name. And I gave the wrong constituency, so I can't get in trouble for talking about these things. I hate the government and I hate most of the MPs I will be working with. I want to do my bit to make the world a better place. Parliament is full of clowns and people in it for themselves. As I look down at my baby daughter sleeping in her travel system on the seat beside me, I promise her that I will do my best to change the world to make it better for her generation.

Anyway, back in 1999, if you remember, I couldn't see, because my glasses were broken in the crash. Charlie, James and I had gone a good couple of miles up the track towards Yarmouth. After falling to my knees with the nastiest Asthma attack I had had in some time, then I saw the ghosts of my dead brother and his lovely girlfriend who died not far from where we sat. They told me about the threat out on the marsh, but they didn't know what it was, and they told me to kiss Charlie, so I did and twice, and it was the best decision I ever made.

However, James disappeared, and while looking for him, I lost Charlie and found Mandy, Sadie and Tom—whose head I'd just seen cut off.

They were coming from the wrong way and claimed not to be my friends and said that I was a horrible person who did things I would never dream of.

When I begged them to turn back towards Yarmouth, they told me that was where they were headed, and I was going the wrong way. However, after coming to an understanding with them that we had all gone mad, because they were not the people I knew, and I was not the person they new. We turned the way they were going. Back towards the train.

I hoped I was wrong about it being the wrong direction, but I wasn't. There was no sign of Charlie or James— which scared the shit out of me—but we did end up back at the train and what scared me more is that after all the time that had passed, there was no help. No emergency services, and even worse, none of the search parties had returned.

The alternate versions of my friends were panicking, the alternate version of Sadie, who was heavily pregnant was shaking and crying as she explained what she saw. Kate, who had been on the ground in labour was gone, there was no sign of Jimmy either. Becky was bleeding out from her badly broken leg. She was screaming incoherently something about people taking her sister and killing Sue, and that Jim was dead.

Mandy was going mad trying to stop Becky from bleeding out with Tom's help while I stood there helplessly as Sadie threw her guts up at what she told me was the sight of Sue's brain splattered over Becky. Despite Becky saying he had died, there was no sign of Jim.

So, you can understand the truth about why I have left it so long to talk about these things and why I left it to the last minute to write my piece. As the head of the company, I was the reason these poor people were put in the situation. Although I have been told these stories many times over the years, it was really hard for me not to go off of the rails when I read Becky's account of how Jimmy died, and Sue was beaten to death by these people who came out of the dark to kidnap Kate and her baby.

Then there was Sharon's account of how Mike's throat was cut because he refused to tell the blonde bitch where Amber was.

There are more deaths and tragedies to come in this story and although I've never killed anyone, I still deep down in my heart feel that they would not have been there if not for me.

I didn't know this stuff at the time, and I was panicking. Apart from Sue and Jim being dead, Georgie, Amber, John, and Jack were still missing, and now James and Charlie could be added to that number.

Hearing Becky's panicked screams in my ear as they tried to help, feeling my breathing erratic and my lungs screaming. Before I knew it, I was on the floor again, struggling with my inhaler. This time I didn't see Dave and Sarah like I thought I might do, and neither was it Charlie who came to my rescue.

It was a dream-like state. The other people around me were gone. There was a figure standing just out of my vision with hair blowing in the wind, watching me lying on the ground. Suddenly, I could see without my glasses as the woman stepped forward. She was around my age, but much prettier than me, she was naked and well-toned with perfect skin and red hair down to her waist.

There was no time to wonder who this person was or whether she was a friend because she was not clearly human. She was like nothing I'd ever seen; she glowed orange in the darkness. She was looking right at me and laughing with a small high-pitched cackle before she spoke softly in words I'll never forget.

'Jessica, Jessica,' she smiled in a patronising tone as my lungs felt ready to burst and my heart seemed like it would fall out of my chest to the floor any second. 'Why fight the pain to stay alive when dying would be so much easier? let it go.'

'H-H' I gasped but could not find the breath to ask her who she was and how she knew my name.

'Oh, dear dear, inhaler not working?' She taunted as I pressed down on it, hoping for a blast of Ventolin but getting nothing at all as I coughed and wheezed.

I could feel the alternate version of Sadie holding me and trying to help however she could while the others tended to Becky, but I couldn't see any of them and they could not see the woman in front of me.

'So many questions' she taunted. 'Where is Charlie? Where is Georgie? Where is James? Where is Jack? And where is Amber, ha ha? Why is no help coming? Why isn't Tom dead now? Who killed Sue, and if dear old Jim is dead as the walking rainbow girl says then where is his body?'

I managed to struggle the words out, 'Do d-do you know where w-where they are?'

I have no idea why I was asking a strange woman— who had come out of the dark and was probably made up in my head—where my friends were. But then she was the one who mentioned them, so she must know.

'Ooh I know dearie,' She smiled patronisingly. 'I just read your mind, but only two of them matter. I already have the boy, Jack. I will find the girl who calls herself Amber and I will burn the two virgins on a fire to appease the lord Satan and laugh as they drown in flames while my power for instant death and mass murder is returned to me.'

'Whoever you are you will harm them over my dead body' I yelled suddenly finding my breath as though the asthma attack had miraculously disappeared.

'Oh, dearie dearie,' she laughed mockingly, coming towards my face as a cold chill on the wind hit me and made my very bones shudder. I stood deadly still as she looked past me to something over my shoulder saying, 'Why would I do it over your dead body when I have a big fire already out on the marshes, and your dead body is over there?'

Following her gaze over my shoulder, I saw something that made me stop in my tracks. My miraculous recovery from my asthma attack was not a recovery.

When I looked back, I saw the alternate versions of Sadie, Mandy, Tom, Becky and another person standing over my lifeless body trying desperately to get me breathing. So this was why my lungs had stopped screaming, and I got my sight back, I was dead.

Trembling with fright, I turned back to the woman to ask more questions only to find that the young redhead was gone and, in her place, stood an old woman. However, it was clearly the same woman. Her skin had become haggard and stretched. It was like one of those awful movies where ghosts or bad monsters are trying to fool living people that they are alive. Then as soon as the living people's back is turned, they become old and ugly to show the audience they are the bad guy.

I say awful, not because I was scared, but because it makes those movies cheap and dumb. I mean it, Hollywood, those type of movies are really crap and boring, so stop making them.

Joking aside, the old woman was terrifying and opened her mouth and in a creek told me, in a voice more terrible than I had ever heard in my life. 'Forget what your brother told you about pubs and motorbikes in heaven. He was lying.

All that's here for you now is to stand here in the cold and the dark where you fell, screaming while nobody hears you until the earth itself is gone. Then you will be left to float, madly haunting the place where you died forever, even when there are no sun and no planet. Just freezing in space until the end of time.

Then she pulled something from thin air. It seemed to be a long pipe which she sparked up with a click of her fingers. As I stood there crying, trembling at the loss of my life and my friends, she puffed a cloud of red sweet- smelling smoke in my face. I'll be honest, I'm a sensible girl and never had the desire to smoke, but whatever that red smoke was, it tasted so lush that I wanted some of the shit myself.

The moment the smoke hit her lungs; the haggard old woman began to change. One more drag on her pipe, and she had turned back into the gorgeous young woman once more.

'You can't smoke this dearie.' She leered 'It's my own creation for me only, and it only works for me.'

'And who are you?' I asked more forcibly than I ever had in my life. I mean, I might as well ask because I was dead already. What would this freaky scary woman who had appeared from nowhere do exactly? Kill me?

At this point, I was just going with the flow. This night could well have been nothing more than one of my nightmares. Things were too strange, a guy losing his head and coming back to life, my friends being hurt or missing.

Usually, my dreams then were as they are now. It was friends and family dying, and not me. In my mind my brother Dave and the lovely Sarah were gone in the real world, but I saw them in my dreams and lost them again in the morning when I woke up. I dreamed about losing my mum who I did really love, without healing the rift which had caused us not to speak for over ten years. I dreamed about my dad dying and everyone having a party because we all hated the racist, homophobic loser. But I never dreamed of myself dying.

The woman smiled at me in a twisted face and said, 'I may as well tell you, because everyone will know me soon enough.' Then she offered her hand and told me in a good impression of Doctor Evil from Austin Powers, 'We are not so different you and I.'

'Really and why is that?' I asked quietly trembling as I took her hand to shake.

'We are both employees of the devil, only you don't realise it yet.'

'Actually, I'm self-employed.' I replied.

'Was self-employed when you were alive,' she corrected, 'Self-employed as a middleman, sorry woman, between the companies you make money on behalf of and the people whose money they take.'

She took another drag on her pipe as I stood speechless at her accusations yet in awe of how much she knew about my life.

'You knock on people's doors, preying on the old and the weak with your smiles, and I think you truly want to believe you are helping them. However, you know in your heart that once anything happens, these companies that you sell for will not pay out when their clients are in need. They take people's hard-earned money and cause them nothing but pain and misery.'

I couldn't speak. She had a point. In some ways she was actually right, apart from the fact I don't allow my staff to sell to vulnerable people who don't understand. We did not sell to over-fifties either. We thought we were helping people buy selling them, what on paper sounded like great policies, but we don't follow up once a sale is made, because the person was no longer our client once their policy started.

How did we know if these companies were actually paying out when our clients needed them to? I felt dreadful as I wondered just how many people had been ripped off and left in trouble because of my aims to help get people employed in our company. Surely the good things I'd done outweighed the bad a million to one. But then maybe those who think they are doing something for the good of others are actually the worst.

But then again finding out that the insurance we had sold to people was dodgy was also one of my worst nightmares.

'See, not so different,' she grinned horribly. 'We are both women who work hard to do the jobs we were meant to do. You mean well but sell dodgy insurance, and you put your heart and soul into your job just like me. Only my job is a little different to yours, and my powers are a little more special.'

'Really? and what makes you so special? And why do you have to burn my friends?' I dared to ask, seeing as it wasn't going to change my fate if I was already dead.

'Well, I have worked hard in my job, cut off from my master with no direction from above or below, but tonight, under the blood moon, our master shall rise from his slumber and restore the powers that were taken from us centuries ago. For hundreds of years, we have manipulated humans into killing themselves with war and terror. Over the past four hundred and fifty years since my birth, with me at the helm, my people have used mind control to mastermind such things as two world wars and many terrorist organisations like the IRA and the British Conservative Party.'

'The Tory party are terrorists?' I asked shocked, 'I don't like them at all, and I think they're the worst thing that ever happened to this country and them losing the last election was a great thing for this country.'

'Funny,' she smiled 'That you don't seem to realise that the current Labour prime minister and his MPs are also under the mind control of my people, and if tonight is unsuccessful, he will continue to drive the country and the United States into war in Afghanistan and Iraq among other places. It doesn't matter who wins as long as humans die.'

'Right, okay,' I told her, stalling as I wondered why she was bothering to tell me all this if I was dead. I was hoping that keeping her talking might put my death on hold a little longer as I saw the others still doing rescue breaths on me.

'I know first aid and so do my friends,' I told her firmly. 'They're only doing rescue breaths so I assume I still have a pulse, meaning I'm not actually dead.'

'Well,' she sneered in a terrifying voice, 'Say they do manage to get you breathing against all the odds, your survival will only last an hour, or two at most once I get my way.'

With her youth regained to my horror, I saw she was joined by an army of dark strangers who had joined her from the shadows, she pointed to the stars.

'When the spell is complete and our powers are regained, we shall strike right away, and in days or less, the world will burn. Only those who can walk in fire as we can, shall be unharmed.'

Her army pointed to the sky and flames shot from their hands. It was the biggest fire I had ever seen. The sky was burning, and so were the marshes around me. All of a sudden, my skin was on fire and the pain was everywhere and nowhere. Then I was floating away as though death had taken me and I was soon way above the earth looking down.

It was not just the marsh burning, and it was not just the sky. Not only was the whole of Norfolk on fire, not only was it the whole of England or Great

Britain or planet earth. The whole of existence was burning. The woman had now begun to grow sharp curling horns from her head, and still, she laughed and laughed untouched as everything that ever existed turned to ash.

I awoke with a sudden intake of air, to find myself surprisingly alive with people standing around.

'Welcome back to the land of the living,' said a voice in my ear. I opened my eyes, expecting to see blurred figures, the best I could hope for without my glasses, but to my surprise, everything was crystal clear.

My breathing was still rapid, and my heart was going ten to the dozen, but I could see them all clearly. Mandy with an unlit cigarette, looking relieved that I was alive, Sadie big and pregnant, smiling at me. Becky looking bedraggled and covered in blood, but alive, and another younger girl. I didn't know the other person. She must have been there all along. The others had gone for help, so maybe she was part of the help.

The stranger, who looked a lot like Amber, didn't stop at saving me. I saw her bend down a few feet away. In my horror I saw Sue laying motionless. There was still a little light from the dying embers of the train, which was several metres away. There was, however, enough light for me to see that Sue was beyond saving. I had never seen anything so horrible in my life as the hole in her head with her brains spilling out.

The strange blonde girl put her hands on Sue's head and closed her eyes tightly and muttered something under her breath.

I sat bolt upright. Her words were strange and mystical, and her voice seemed to come from somewhere far away. As she did this, a strange glow seemed to come from Sue.

My eyes must have been lying to me, because what they saw was Sue's blood and brains oozing back towards the hole in her head. Even the blood and brains on Becky's clothes started to float away from her toward Sue.

What was I seeing? This sort of thing only happened in books and movies. I didn't know how she was doing it, but this girl was putting Sue back together. The hole was closed, and her injuries fixed, but just when I thought the miracle was going to happen and that Sue was going to breathe, the girl stopped muttering and looked to the sky, then to the group of us who were looking on, and she shook her head with tears in her eyes.

'I can't d–do it,' she stuttered. 'She's too broken and too long dead. The soul is already gone across the bridge, and she has been welcomed by her family and the families of those she saved when she was a nurse in the Korean War. So many people's lives saved by this humble lady, and a single blow to her head took hers, and even my magic can't save her.'

'I'm sorry,' I said, finding my voice as I choked back the tears. She turned slowly to look at me uneasily and said nervously, 'Hello, I'm Jenny. I fixed your friend's leg.' She nodded to Becky, who I had suddenly realised was standing by me on her leg that had been badly broken and bleeding.

All I could say was 'How? How? WHAT??' I heard

Mandy stutter, 'If we hadn't all just seen her do it, I would be asking if these guys were on drugs.'

'Maybe it would be better for you guys if you just pretend you are!' she replied to Mandy.

'Now,' she told me directly. 'You were going to die, but the spirits told me that many people need you alive, so I had to do something very risky to save your life.' She took a quick breath and continued before I could ask what the hell was going on.

'You were so near death that you had an out-of-body experience, and I know what you saw, and I know, that woman in your vision, she was not really here, but she was in your head, and she is dangerous. It's her people who have taken your friend and her baby. It's them that killed this lady.' She nodded to Sue. 'Your friends Jack and Amber have been selected and groomed to be here this night. She crashed the train so she could grab them from it, and they got Jack by snatching him the moment your backs were turned.'

I tried to butt in quickly, but she continued, 'Amber, however, was taken by another double agent loyal to the child known as the Redhead Witch, who was trying to keep her safe, but he met with an accident.' She paused 'Which partly is my fault, so we won't mention it. But she is out there on her own and I need to get back to her once I've helped you.'

'Where are the rest of my team?' I asked, followed by Mandy who asked, 'And our team.'

'The world is in meltdown,' she breathed. 'They screwed the whole of reality, and this reality has crashed into the next one and now there's two of everyone running around out here. Including me and…' She turned to me and said, 'Including the woman you saw in your dream. Either way, you try to run, one of her will be there.'

'Okay,' I breathed, 'If this is not all a dream and it is all true, is there any way we can put this all right?'

After a moment's silence as she was clearly trying to think, but she smiled weakly. 'I am the only rebel against a barely apposed army of evil witches and wizards, and I can't fight them if they get what they want. However, if your friend Amber stays hidden and doesn't give herself to them, then we may have a chance, but we need to seek help in the Freaks Village.'

We all took a collective breath and said, 'The Freaks Village. What the fuck is that?'

Chloe

For those of you who are observant, you will realise that like Katie, I was not one of the people on the train at the start of the story. In fact, just like her, I didn't come in until part two when my sister Helen found James wandering alone in the dark by the railway.

So, now you're wondering who we are and what we were doing out in the dark miles from anywhere with our faces covered and our voices sounding like men?

Well, there are many things in this world that normal everyday people either don't see or choose to ignore. One of those is freaks of nature—people who are different. Many freaks can bleed into society and walk about in daylight like a normal person without having to worry. That's because some can hide their differences, others, however, do not hide their differences so easily.

The governments of the world know about us but try to keep us quiet. That's how a lot of us who can't be seen in the light, end up claiming disability benefits, or working from home so that they stay home all day and are never seen.

However, if you are vigilant in your day-to-day life, you will find that we don't all hide away in the day until dark. For example, my big sister Karen and I both have night-time jobs in a supermarket in Norwich where we unpack deliveries on the night shift. The delivery drivers know us and our differences from everyday people very well. This is because they are freaks too. In fact, the night is full of us just going about our jobs and minding our own business and hurting nobody.

So, what classes a person as a freak? Well, it's really all about being different from a normal person, it can be physical, or it can be the possession of a strange ability. Two examples of this are friends of mine. One is a girl who can move things with her mind like the girl from Roald Dahl's book Matilda, and the other is a seven-foot-tall walking,

talking, very intelligent sasquatch—also known as Bigfoot —so you can see why she doesn't get out much.

The Freaks' Christmas Village is not just a Christmas village, in fact when it's not Christmas it's just a holiday village. It's a huge camp hidden away from the road and the railway, while still within walking distance. That being said, I will get in trouble if I give the exact distance, so I will add that walking distance for me is one hundred

miles.

When I say holiday village, I don't mean like a holiday village where you pay £150 per person per week to hire a caravan or the same per night for a hotel. It's more like a music festival, but without the rubbish left after. It's £1 per person per night if you bring your own tent, and £2 if you hire one. When you consider that there are 20,000 of them living in Norfolk and space for 100,000. At a minimum of £1 per person at capacity, the camp fees make an income of £1.4 million over the two weeks at Christmas. I bet the landowner puts most of that in an offshore account.

Like I say, it's not just for Christmas, because the village is there all year round, but it was the start of the millennian celebrations on the night in question.

It was my first year of visiting, and I was young. For all my size and my booming deep voice, under that mask, if you believe me, was a sixteen-year-old girl who had gone away on holiday, away from her parents for the first time and I was rather scared that I would be the one to give away the secret of the Freaks Village and I was terrified of putting a foot wrong. That's why I was so against taking James back with us.

For those of you thinking that I can't be that bothered about the secret, seeing as I've just written a great deal about it. I have come with age to realise that the human race is so closed-minded that nobody will actually believe me. Plus, if you go looking for the place, you will not find it.

So, you may or may not ask what we were doing outside of the camp. Well, we have an understanding. With such a big event going on more are more people were needed to keep watch over the camp, especially because on a full moon the werewolves and vampires leave the camp and go off into the fields to let the wolves run wild where there is nobody for them to hurt.

Our kind (The girls who James met) volunteer to keep watch outside of the circle to warn the vampires of unexpected people out on the marsh.

We were not far from the train when it exploded. Everything from the moment that train had gone up in smoke was mayhem. There were as many of us out there

on the marshes as there were people from the train. We wanted to stay hidden, but at the same time we could protect them from the wolves as best we could if they got through.

Obviously, the group headed towards Acle must have been distracted by something, because regrettably Sadie, who has already told of what happened to her, was bitten.

I felt like the others that the best thing to do would have been to reunite James with his friends. We looked for them, but we only looked from one side of the track. My theory is that if reports of a crack in the world are to be believed, then they must have simply been sat on the other side of it.

Apart from vampires and werewolves, we had not been expecting to have company on the marshes that night. The pagans obviously would have been fine, as long as they didn't know about us, and we kept out of their way. The wizards and witches, however, had openly threatened people from the freak's village telling them to stay away unless they wanted to die.

I didn't want to die because I was on holiday, and I didn't want it ruined.

Basically, us taking James to the camp was the last resort for his safety, because we weren't going to let him die.

I was scared of the reaction we might get from the other freaks when we got there, if anything. I didn't want us to be in trouble if they thought us showing him the camp was not the right thing to do. I was also worried about how close and casual my big sister Helen was with James. She was acting as though we could all remain friends, once this situation was over. It was my feeling that any continued friendship after that night would have been impossible. How can a normal young man and woman who can't go out in public without her face covered truly be friends? I didn't want to be the one passing the tissues to my sister when it all ended in tears. Strangely it worked and unreliably we have remained friends. In fact, James is here right now.

For a bit better visual description of the camp. The walls around it are made of canvas and are three and a half miles long making it 3 square miles. Much bigger than the famous Glastonbury music festival. However, that doesn't have walls.

Inside the high walls, there were several big-top circus-style tents on the far side. Inside were all the shops and bars and so on. On the nearest side to where we entered is where the personal sleeping tents were pitched just behind one of the four reception areas.

After booking ourselves in at reception, which was unmanned, we made our way towards the centre of the village.

Usually, it was full of people relaxing, but there was an air of panic to the place. It might have seemed to James who had never been there before that it was the usual hustle and bustle. But for us it seemed like there was a huge panic going on. Helen pulled someone aside and demanded to know what was going on. The person replied in short. 'Meeting now in the centre, everyone, the camp is under attack from the wizards.'

Amber

I opened my eyes and looked around. There was a blonde woman about my height and possibly my age too. She'd done something, something to the troll. He'd fallen to the ground. That must have been the crash that shook the earth. How did this woman get here and how had she taken out the troll?

'Well, don't thank me for saving your life too much,' she scoffed sarcastically. 'Not like I just took out a troll that was going to kill you or nothing.'

'You killed him.' I yelled. 'You're one of them. The people he told me about. The ones that are trying to destroy mankind. He was trying to help, and you killed him.'

'Wait… what?' she shrugged, looking me in the eye with an open mouth. 'He's a troll. They are on the side of the people who are trying to destroy humans.'

'He was a rebel.' I screamed at her. 'I asked him to kill me, so you guys couldn't catch me, and I'm not going to let you…'

'Shush!' she commanded. 'I'm not here to kill you. I'm a rebel too! It would have helped one hell of a lot if I'd known he was and maybe I wouldn't have shocked him so hard.'

There was a loud groan and a deep grunt from the direction where Ulskane had fallen. 'I'm sorry, troll,' she called in his direction. 'I didn't mean to hurt you, and please don't stand on me.'

'Who the hell are you?' I demanded.

'Jenny,' she said with a smile. 'Not to be confused with the other Jenny. There's two of us in the resistance.'

'Well, it is a common name.' I shrugged. 'With a large number of people it's likely that there will be two people called Jenny.'

'No… two of us in the resistance', she grinned, 'and yeah, we are both called Jenny.'

I took in a long breath, 'I banged my head in the crash, right?'

'You may well have done.' she beamed with eery eyes. 'But before you say it, this is still real.'

In the confusion of everything and never really believing anything that I'd seen in the last hour was real, I almost forgot to question some of the other strange things. I mean, what on earth had she been doing out in the middle of nowhere? How was it that I could see her in the dark, never mind the fact that she just took out what was essentially a giant without physically touching him.

She looked at me almost playfully with wide eyes. She wasn't like you imagine a witch flying on a broomstick. Like me, she was blonde and not very tall. Again, like me, she didn't look unhealthy but seemed to be one sausage roll away from being chubby. Not fat, just chubby, but she was prettier than I was, like most people with a face. 'Get that thing out of your mouth.' She scorned, pulling at my cigarette. 'My people, they push stuff like that on you. They lost their powers, which they used to kill people, so they found other ways to do it with more entertainment value.'

I frowned, 'What? Why would your people do that?'

'Fun,' she shrugged. 'they're horrible sadistic murderers with a lot of time on their hands, so they pray on human weaknesses like addictions so they can watch you suffer slowly and enjoy watching your health decline until you die. Average human beings are stupid, you can't help it.'

'So, whatever you are, you're better than us?'

'Not really.' She shrugged a second time. She smiled and took my cigarette and took a deep puff. 'Yuck' she laughed, throwing it aside. 'You need a big cup of hot coffee and some fizzy drink to keep your energy up.'

'Yeah, because there's obviously a coke machine and a kettle just over there in the field.' I half laughed. 'No there isn't,' she replied with a sniff.

'Well then, no coffee or cola for us.' I turned right away to walk off in the direction where I hoped I may find Jack. With the troll now lying on the floor, seemingly unable to move, and me not having anything sharp or explosive to kill myself with, I guess risking the world was the only way.

No sooner had I turned to storm off than I walked into something very hard and brightly lit up. *No way!* It was a flipping fizzy drink machine in the middle of the field.

'Believe I'm a witch now?' she grinned.

'I didn't ever think you weren't.' I gasped.

She dropped her head on its side and smiled.

'Your thoughts said differently.'

Sceptically, I thumped my hand on the rectangular button to select a can of Iron Bru. Nothing happened, and she burst out laughing. 'It's a drink machine. You have to put money in it.' Smiling, I put my hand in my pocket and took out a 50p coin and put it in the slot. I heard it drop and pressed the button again. Still nothing. I pressed every button, but still nothing.

'You didn't expect a working one, did you?' She giggled. 'I'm a witch. I don't need a machine to get you drink.' There was a small pop and a can of drink appeared in each of her hands. She offered one to me and I took it without question and took a gulp.

To my surprise, rather than a cold can of pop, the liquid was hot, sweet and warming. Just the right temperature for me. 'Whatever your body wants will come out of the can.' She shrugged.

'I have more questions for you' I trembled. 'Is what the troll said true? Are there people out there trying to raise devil? Do they want to kill me and Jack and are we really the only virgins?'

'Yes, but it's more complicated than the trolls' understanding.' She sniffed casually conjuring a large tissue out of thin air. She took it and blew her nose with a snort, then threw it up a good few feet and pointed at it with her finger, causing it to disappear. 'So, if you're a witch, how did you catch a cold?' 'Did you go to school?' She asked seriously.

'When I felt like it.' I grinned. 'But it wasn't Mrs Cackle's academy or Hogwarts or nothing like that.'

'Those places don't exist,' she grunted. 'But, basically, there are these things in the air called germs and us witches and wizards do catch them. I caught mine from my boyfriend's mum.'

My eyes opened wide as I turned to look at her. 'You have a boyfriend?'

'Of course, I do!' She said with a twisted sneer. 'I may be a witch, but that's just one part of me. I'm also a nineteen nearly twenty-year-old woman with sexual needs, just like anyone else. Plus, I love the bones of my Terry, he's a great guy.'

'So, is he one of your people?' I asked, continuing to walk quickly, not knowing where exactly we were going.

'God no.' she spat out with laughter. 'He's a normal human being, just like most people. I'm supposed to be getting in with the humans just while our kind are looking for a way to regain our powers of death. I don't want to have that power I don't want to kill normal humans. In fact, I'd rather be one.'

I looked at her with an air of scepticism. 'You can summon things like never-ending drinks from thin air and you want to give that up to be human?'

'Maybe not,' she shrugged, 'I suppose not being able to fly would be inconvenient, too.'

Hang on, if she could fly, why was she down here with me, walking to wherever it was we were going to? When I asked, she said something about there being others up there flying around looking for us. 'We can't get there too fast either.' she whispered. 'If we get there too fast and they catch you, it will give them more time. We need them to be in a hurry. They are more likely to fuck the whole thing up, if they haven't already done it, by crashing two worlds into one another.'

'Again, what?' I yelled, nearly gagging on my drink. 'Some complicated spell? I'm old enough and experienced enough to know how they did it, but I'm not sure if it was on purpose. Two versions of reality bumped into each other. People are spilling over from one side to the other. It could be that they did it to gather reinforcements.'

She paused to sneeze, conjuring up a hanky for the briefest of seconds, then waving it into thin air again, continuing to talk as though nothing happened. 'Maybe to them, ridding one world of humanity is better than nothing at all.'

'Why are you different to them.' I asked bluntly. 'If they want to kill humans, but you don't, surely there are more like you.

'I see why you would say there might be.' She nodded 'I've never let my secret slip, so others may be doing the same. But there's something special about me. I'm not just trying to stop them, because I fell in love with a human, and don't want him dead.'

She paused and took a long drink from her can. Then she looked me in the eye. 'I know this is a lot to take in. You didn't know we existed an hour ago, and here I am trying to get your head around it.'

'Well, I get that they need two virgins to make their spell work.'

'And a newborn baby and among several other things which the troll probably didn't know to tell you.'

'The troll!' I gasped, remembering that we had left him behind. 'He was nice he was trying to help me.'

'By killing you?'

'Yes, if I'm dead, then they can't have their virgin.'

'You're a brave woman,' she breathed 'Braver than me, but I have a better idea on how to get rid of the whole virgin problem. You could, you know, just shag somebody and then it wouldn't be a problem.'

Her words and advice about shagging somebody would come back to me later that night and would, in fact, be the thing that saved my life.

We walked for some time, maybe half an hour, and we talked as though the conversation she and I were having was normal.

'I did a spell on you,' She told me. 'They can't hear you or see you now. Or me for that matter.'

I was forced to believe what she told me, because I had nothing to prove her wrong with.

She gave me all of the history of her people, but I'm sure Kate or one of the others will have given you some of the details. Also, we have said a lot about it in part one. I don't want to go over the whole thing again if they have already said it. The troll also told me about a lot in part two.

Basically, the story goes that the devil, not god, created the world. But god took credit for it, but the devil wanted it back, so he created the evil witches to destroy it. Then, God or whatever being it was who claimed to have created the earth made his own version of the witches to fight the ones that were using their magic to kill people.

'Of course, all history is just what they want us to hear' She smiled. 'But the basis of it is that we are bad witches, and the others are good two kinds were fighting for a long time.

Then, since the dawn of humanity, there had been this huge standoff and power struggles. Yes, I know it all started with a simple train crash and it's getting very complicated.

So, in the late fifteen hundreds or sixteen hundreds, one of the two. The last two of the resistance were killed, but before they died, they found a way to stop the bad guys forever and send them back into the shadows.

Tonight, was the night they were planning to do the spell under the blood moon and would try to raise the devil and get their powers back.

Jenny wasn't clear on everything that was going on, and here is why. 'Well firstly, I'm only nineteen, so I'm not in on everything that's going on.'

'Fair enough,' I nodded. 'Everything I told you is from my world or my dimension. The other me is from your world but I came over from another dimension to help so I was not involved in it, but I assume the plans are similar to what was going on in my world.'

'So, there are two of everyone from the train running around out here in the dark?' She nodded to confirm, adding, 'Although they are not completely the same people. There are two women, one in your world and one in mine who were once twin sisters, but one died, a different one. And you're not the Virgin they were going to sacrifice either.'

'Other me isn't a virgin then.' I laughed. 'At least one of me is getting some.'

'Believe it or not, you're married in my world to the very boy that you're trying to save now.

Then there was this child they called the redheaded witch. Something I didn't understand. This child was only a rumour and if she was real, then she was lost somewhere, but somehow didn't matter as long as she lived to be eighteen. They found a person with genes of their enemy and one of them bred with her to create a child. The rebirth of the enemy could then be a second way to bring their powers to kill humans back.

'If I'm right wherever she is, she is nearly eleven years old, so even if we're successful tonight, then we could be fucked again in seven years if she turns eighteen without knowing who she is, and even if she does, one eighteen-year-old newbie can't stop them.' 'It's kinder to find the poor kid and slit her throat while she sleeps so the spell can't be broken.' She sighed. 'But they would have made others.'

'Well, I think we need to get tonight over with first before we think about seven years' time, don't you think?' I told her confidently, adding, 'I'm not sure I'm gonna be alive in seven hours, let alone seven years if they want to sacrifice me tonight.'

'You will not die tonight,' she told me confidently, as she paused to take one more drink.

'You can't promise that.' I retorted.

'I can if you look at me.' She grinned.

'What do you mean?' I grimaced. 'Look harder.' She smiled. 'Who do you see?' 'I see you I suppose.' I grunted back.

'But who do I look like to you?'

'You do seem familiar.' I shrugged.

'Well, I bloody well do. Don't you ever look in the mirror?'

'Well, you don't look like me, do you.' I scoffed, 'I may not have a mirror at home, but there's no way I'm as pretty as you are.'

'Wrong.' She said simply. 'When I first touched you on the shoulder, I copied your biomolecular structure. I'm an exact copy of you.'

'I don't believe you.' I said, looking her up and down. 'I'm fatter than you for starters.'

'Really? Are you?' She asked bluntly, putting her head on the side. 'But I look like this.'

I thought something dramatic was going to happen and she would turn into a completely different person with dark hair and green eyes or something. But all that happened was her hair grew a little longer and a shade brighter and she grew around three inches taller, and her belly only slimmed down a fraction. Yet she just seemed to be a taller me.

I laughed, 'You don't seem much different.'

'Well, I guess you and I don't look too different from each other, but I can only be something I've touched like a boyfriend, for example.

She spontaneously turned into a scrawny young man with spiky hair and glasses.

'Well, somebody's punched above their weight in your relationship.' I teased, to which she sighed. 'I know! But I just count myself incredibly lucky that he can't see he's dating a minger.'

I was actually meaning the other way around, but moving on as she turned back into me, she plucked something out of thin air. It was a cigarette lighter. Before I could question her motives, she took my hand in her spare hand and clicked the lighter, holding the flame against my hand.

It hurt enough for me to shout out, 'Fuck you, you crazy bitch.' Luckily as I say she had told me that she put a spell on us to stop us from being heard. The pain was enough to bring tears to my eyes. She may have done a crazy thing, but I was sure she had a reason for it, because she apologised straight away and blew on it. Immediately the burn disappeared along with the throbbing and as I gawped at the healed burn in shock, she handed me the lighter, smiling. 'Now do it to me.'

Planning to get her back good and proper, I took the lighter and I clicked it and held on to her with all I had pressing her towards the flame. I had thought it wouldn't hurt her if she was a witch, but I was wrong. She was genuinely shaking in pain but trying not to show it. Then just when I thought I'd given enough, her clothes suddenly caught light, and she burst into flames. The look on her face was a brave grimace of somebody who was suffering incredibly. I didn't know how to help her, she was burning fast, and I had no water. Why did she not summon some water to put the fire out?

After a moment of screaming, she smiled at me and began to scream. 'I'm melting, I'm melting. in all the world who would have thought you could defeat me.' And with that, leaving me gobsmacked, she just crumpled to dust.

I was frozen with shock. Surely this was some sick joke. But of course, in the sixteen hundreds they burned witches at the stake to kill them. But why would she suddenly ask me to do that to her.

I pondered this as I stood staring down at the pile of ashes that was left of her where she had stood. Then out of nowhere, came a sound like the growl of a fierce dog or wolf or something. It scared the shit out of me something terrible. I spun around to see this huge foul beast running with something in its mouth. It looked like a person. We now know it was Sadie. A tap on my shoulder made me jump with fright a second time.

I spun back on my heels and there was Jenny, alive and well, having come back from the dead after just being burned in front of my eyes. She just carried on talking as though what I had just witnessed was normal.

'So, I think the plan is to burn you in some sort of Wicker-Man type scenario.' She breathed before taking another huge gulp of drink and then a deep breath and continuing before I could interject. 'So, we find their base, and at the last minute you hand yourself in and when it comes to the burning, I rescue you. I take your place disguised as you and do that. I'm not the virgin they want, so the spell will not work.'

This sounded like a good plan, but something in my mind was nagging. I walked silently, trying to think what it was and then it hit me. 'But what about the virgin from your world? Surely if you came from the other side and were planning something similar, surely your world has virgins, too. What if they get to her or him? That makes our chances futile.' Then I remembered what I'd just seen. 'Oh yeah, and there was a wolf eating somebody over there. I'm guessing it was with your people.'

'Werewolf' She shrugged. 'Nothing to do with us, but they come out here on the full moon to lessen the chances of harming people.'

'That one didn't succeed.' I trembled, 'It had a person in its mouth.'

'I'm sorry if it was one of your friends,' she breathed a deep sigh. 'There is no virgin from my side of the divide.'

'Well, if there wasn't a virgin to sacrifice in your dimension, how do you know that what they're planning is the same thing.'

'There was.' She grunted, then looked away. When she looked back there was a tear in her eye. 'I was supposed to be the one who captured them, but I was going to save her, like I am you.'

'What happened?' I asked softly.

She groaned. 'I followed her and her sister, the pregnant girl who was meant to give her baby to the devil. I would have grabbed them and taken them to safety when they got off the train. They were such a lovely pair of sisters, Becky and Kate.'

'Becky and Kate as in Becky and Kate, as in the same Becky and Kate from my world who pretend to hate each other. Just different incarnations?'

She nodded. 'Only their train crashed harder than yours and they died.'

My mouth fell open. They hadn't died in the world, I knew. Well, Becky was injured and Kate in labour. I felt awful for them and their families, even though I never met them.

'Shit,' she said suddenly, looking up at the sky. 'What the fuck is going on up there?'

'What' up where?'

'Up there,' she told me, pointing to the sky.

'No time to explain if I don't come back hand yourself in… And one more thing.' She breathed with a vain pulsing in her head. 'One of my people infiltrated your group. You know him as John and there is also an informant from my side. An older woman who lost her husband many years ago.

Without another word, she took off and shot into the sky like Superman to sort out whatever shit was going on up there.

To be continued ………

Jessica 2

That weird flying witch woman Jenny was taking us all to the place she called the freaks village. She thought they could help us. She took us one by one, and she put me on her back first.

Thankfully, the whole flying bit was over in seconds. It was so fast I didn't have time to be frightened and piss myself, so I just pissed myself. Only kidding I shit myself too, well at least I thought I did but when we landed, I was clean and dry.

We landed by this big black wall, made out of some sort of massive fence stretching as far as the eye could see. That was another point, I could see, despite my glasses being broken all night.

'I can see.' I gasped.

'Yep, fixed your glasses,' Jenny told me off handily. 'Are you some kind of magical doctor or something? '

'Nothing of the sort,' she replied, 'I'm a very accomplished witch.'

'How do you become a witch?'

'You don't become the type of witch I am without being born as one. So, don't go getting any ideas of trying to fly or anything because you will never be able to do that.'

'Well, I'm really thankful for you saving my life' I smiled. 'Just lucky that there was a good witch just floating around ready to save my life. Or did you know this was all going to happen?'

'Well, it's very complicated.' she said quickly, 'There are several different plains of reality and several different versions of each of us and two of them have hit each other. Somewhere out there there's another me who's not very good at magic….' She casually flicked her finger and a wooden picnic table appeared with a cup and plate and she nudged me towards it to sit down. '…and another you who runs a sales company only unlike you she's an asshole to be polite.'

'Another me?'

She nodded, 'Two of everyone apart from those that have died. There were enough people out here to fill Wembley stadium twice over and now we can double that. Not just witches though, there are a lot of innocent pagans about, as well as the freaks, vampires and wolves.'

I was about to ask her something when she raised her hand to stop me. 'I'll answer more questions once I've got the others. Now eat your dinner and put your coat on.' She told me turning away to leave. 'Oh' she said, turning back 'The cup and plate will fill with anything you need and those used hankies in your handbag…' She pointed a finger at it. 'Now clean.' And without a word she shot into the sky.

With more and more things buzzing around in my head, it was hard to think. Especially when a gorgeous meal appeared on my plate in front of me. She clearly knew I was a veggie lover. I've been a vegetarian ever since I moved out of my parents' house. Not a preachy vegetarian and I'd never tell you what to eat but I don't like eating animals. I'm not going as far as to be a vegan though.

With everything going on, I think in my mind I had actually died, and this was some sort of weird limbo where I could try to save my friends somehow. I must have died back at the first asthma attack when I saw my dead brother Dave and the gorgeous Sarah who died all those years ago. That would explain Charlie kissing me, then disappearing and James going too. I could have been in a coma I suppose, and Charlie and James had really gone for help. These other people were just made up in my head.

Obviously, I'm alive in 2019, so it wasn't what I was thinking, but you have to understand that it was how I was rationalising it. All I could do I suppose is do what she said and eat up as my tummy was growling. I hoped she was going to feed the others too.

The knife and fork she left me seemed a bit big for my hands. My glasses kept slipping. My white winter coat, which I had left with Jimmy had by some form of magic come back to me and was keeping me warm, but it seemed loose. I ate hungrily, but my tummy filled with much more ease than normal. I was struggling to finish the veggie burger and salad as I took sips of drink. My drink seemed to alternate between strong hot coffee and cold orange juice.

Feeling a sneeze coming on, I reached in my coat pocket and found a clean hankie and smothered it instinctively. Some-how my white, red dotted hanky seemed to have got so big that I struggled even with both hands, especially with my sleeves being so long. Before I got to wipe my nose, I felt something more pressing. My stomach was about to explode. It rumbled for a few seconds as I tried to catch my breath, but you know what it's like when it reaches the point of no return. I projectile vomited all over my clean hanky. It was a mixture of coffee and lumps of undigested veggie burger and bread. Another breath and a second round all over my coat and trousers.

Head spinning, I fell to the ground with a thump, knocking the remains of the burger and salad flying with my elbow. I hit the ground with a thump, luckily; I didn't break my glasses again. I lay on the floor breathing hard, trying to get my bearings.

What the hell was going on? My boots were sliding off, my skirt was loose, my leggings and top were too big, my stomach just could not hold anything in, and there was a thick blanket of hair. My ponytail had been long enough for me to sit on for about the last six months, but now it was below my feet.

Jenny had said there might be side effects from saving me. If only she knew now what was happening.

Becky

It was not the original plan for me to write in this volume because my sister and I have been taking turns. However, she was not there to see this and the others who were apart from Jessie were not there to tell either.

I'm not going to go into where I am in my personal life as others have because you're bored of it, and we will save it for the end of part four.

I had been lying on the floor more time than I could remember, unable to move with my leg hanging off. I wanted to die, so that I didn't have to put up with the hurt anymore. I didn't know who those people were, but they came out of the dark and they took my sister and they left me to bleed. But before that they killed a good woman. Sue was stern, and she was misunderstood, but she was calm and caring and she saved my life. For that, I will be forever grateful.

The images of them smashing her head open as she tried to protect Kate and I will never leave me until the day I die. I just lay there crying and waiting for life to leave me. I had drifted off, hoping that it was for the last time.

No more pain please, not physical or emotional. Then there were voices. Jessie, Mandy, Sadie and some guy who was familiar, but I could not place him.

Mandy and Sadie looked alarmed and then straight at me and they were bent over trying to help me, but behind them, I saw Jessie fall to her knees clearly in distress. Then out of nowhere, there was this girl with blonde hair standing above me. She smiled down at me and whispered. 'Rebecca, it's going to be fine, sweetheart.'

'Are you a paramedic?' I wheezed, to which she replied 'No, I'm something much better, but be aware I don't have any form of medical training so don't sue me.'

I felt her warm hands on my broken leg. She closed her eyes and held my leg tightly. I didn't know what she was doing, but I could feel things moving around. It was like the bone was healing itself. Or not, she was doing it. It seemed to be taking a great effort from the expression on her face. I was in such a state of bad health that it hadn't hit me at first that people cannot do this sort of thing. Broken bones take months to heal if they even heal properly at all. How was she doing it? Actually, I don't care. She was doing it; she was my new favourite person. Mandy and Sadie's mouths dropped open so far that they both dropped their cigarettes on the floor.

That was another strange thing. Mandy gave up smoking months ago and Sadie, well, I wasn't sure I'd ever seen her smoking, but there was something else about Sadie. Where had she been hiding that big pregnant tummy of hers, and if she was pregnant, what the hell was she doing smoking?

'There you are all done.' The strange girl smiled, adding, 'If we all live through tonight, you'll play rugby for England on that leg.'

Instead of thanking you, I murmured, 'Will we win the World Cup?' She grinned and shook her head. 'You put up a good fight, but you lose to South Africa in the semi-final.'

She was already standing up, and she took a look at Sue lying there dead on the grass. I leapt up and hugged Mandy as the strange woman moved on to help Jessie, who now seemed to be in desperate trouble. Mandy just stood there motionless, looking from me to the train and my leg, and then she pushed me away from her.

'Why did you do that, Mandy?' I whimpered, feeling really hurt, that after everything we'd been through, she pushed me away. 'Well, if you can't admit you love me after all this, then what is the point?'

She just stood there, motionless again. I felt an arm on my shoulder and to my surprise, it was Sadie who whispered in my ear with her sexy Spanish accent. 'Sweetie, I don't know what went on here. I hope you're okay, but I assure you she is not your girlfriend, and we are not who you think we are.'

I looked at her sideways with a confused smile and asked her what she meant. She looked down at the ground, a tear formed in her eye.

'Where I come from, this be true. You are you, but you and Mandy are not a thing. And...' She stopped and gulped. 'I just stood by helpless while you and your sister Kate died in each other's arms.'

'Kate's been taken by these people.' I cried. 'Jimmy's dead. They murdered Sue. John went after them, but he's probably dead too.'

Sadie took me in both arms and hugged me so tight, I could feel her baby kicking me in the tummy. 'I don't know how, but we will help you.' She whispered. 'But please tell me who is that girl who fixed your leg and how did she do that?'

I stepped back and stared at her as I felt in my pockets to see if I had a clean hanky to dry my face off from all the crying. (I didn't. It was used but beggars can't be choosers.)

'She's not with you?'

Sadie shook her head as she wiped her own eyes with a tissue then lit up another cigarette. 'What are you doing!' I yelled in disgust. 'Smoking is bad enough for you, let alone for your unborn baby.'

She looked at me like I was crazy taking a large drag. 'But these are prescription cigarettes.' She huffed. 'I get them free on the NHS because they are good for the baby to help it grow to be healthy.

Disclaimer – Cigarettes are disgusting smelly cancer sticks and do not help babies to grow.

However, she passed me the packet as proof, and it confirmed everything she said.

'For optimal health of your child, we recommend that you smoke at least forty a day'

Mandy meanwhile, had gone over to where the strange woman who healed my leg was working hard to save Jessie who looked in some real trouble. She obviously had tried to use her inhaler thing. It was her asthma, but she was out cold on the floor and for all we knew at the time she was dead.

The strange blonde woman was on the floor with her, and she started breathing into her mouth like rescue breaths. 'I'm not sure what I'm doing!' She cried between breaths. 'If I try to use my powers, I might do her more harm than good.'

We all just stood there stunned, not knowing what any of us could do to help. She seemed to try many different things, but Jessie was not responding at all. After a while, she turned to us in desperation and spoke. 'She is not going to live and there is only one thing I can try to bring her back and I might make things very bad for her.'

The three of us looked to one another and then back to her. 'I'm sure she would rather live with whatever happens than die here.' I called out.

The girl nodded at me, and she stopped working on Jessie for a second and took two deep breaths. Then she put her hands under Jessie's top onto her boobs and screwed her eyes tight, as though she was either focusing or in deep pain.

Sparks flew from her hands and her face glowed red as Jessie lit up like a lightbulb and we all jumped back in shock.

There was a moment where we all just glared ahead of us in hope. There was a collective sigh of relief as Jessie took her first rattling breath.

All of us ran over to hug this magical stranger who had seemingly come from nowhere to save our lives. She, however, had no time for hugs. She stood up looking weary as though saving Jessie had zapped her energy. She took a can of drink from what seemed to be out of thin air and took a long swig. Then she wiped her face and nose with a hanky that she seemed to pull out of thin air as she walked quickly back to Sue.

'What about Jimmy?' I pleaded, nodding to the spot where he had lain. 'He was over there. He was burned and he had cancer, but he didn't pass away that long ago.

She looked at the place where I had nodded, and her eyes searched up and down then she smiled. 'Well, the good news is I can at least try to help your friend with his problems, but there is some better news if you want to hear it.'

'Well, firstly, who are you? and how did you just save me and Jessie?'

'First answer, Jenny.' She smiled happily, taking my hand to shake. 'Second answer, no time to explain it all. And three, I might be able to help your friend with his burns, and his cancer, because he's not there. He's walked off, so clearly not dead.'

That was when Jess opened her eyes. So, you will already have read what happened here. How Jenny tried to save Sue but could not.

Jenny explained something about having found Amber and having sent her somewhere and she needed to get back and help her, because of the same bad people who took Kate. Then she told us that the best place we could go to get help was from some

a place called the Freaks Village.

I was as confused as you probably are by this point. As you can tell, none of this stuff happens in the real world. I put this all down to the fact that I was dying, and this was a hallucination.

Jenny told us that she knew of the Freaks Village but didn't know the freaks personally, but they were people with a range of strange conditions that meant they couldn't be themselves in public. They had a permanent holiday camp hidden on the other side of the marsh, but it was full for Christmas, and we might be able to find help there.

'Only problem for you guys is that it's four miles away from here.' A playful grin came across her face. 'But we have fun ways of fast transport.'

She took Jess in her arms and all four of us gasped as the pair of them lifted off of the ground.

There was a twinkle in her eyes as she told us all,

'You may need a sick bag, as I can fly faster than a jumbo jet.' Then she winked at Mandy and Sadie and teased. 'Speeds may vary depending on size. Flying while pregnant is not advised, but these are special circumstances.'

It all happened so fast. They shot up into the sky like superman with Lois Lane. I could hear Jessie screaming in terror.

A few minutes passed. I sat there rather awkwardly on the ground, looking from Sadie to Mandy, and I mopped my eyes and face and blew my nose. It was clear these two ladies were also sick with colds.

'You next, rainbow stick insect.' Came Jenny's voice from behind me. I felt her grab me from behind and my stomach dropped down somewhere past my toes, making me want to vomit everything I ate that day. 'Back in a minute, ladies.' She called down to the others.

I don't even remember what happened in our brief flight. I screwed my eyes tightly shut until it was over. I hate flying in a plane, let alone some random woman picking me up. It was not something science could explain. I felt a rush of wind in my hair, but I didn't dare look down out of fear. Thankfully, soon enough I felt my feet touch the ground and as I opened my eyes, I stumbled and fell to the ground.

'You'll be fine, you did well.' Jenny called down to me as she took to the sky once more, pointing towards a huge canvas wall around Twenty metres away. 'I left your friend over there. She's got food and drink for you. Look after her. I'll be back in a minute.' Then in a whoosh, she was gone.

I stumbled dizzily in the direction she pointed in. There was a large canvas wall as I said, but without a torch, I could not see it well. In the light of the moon, I could just about make out a doorway in the high wall.

'Jessie, where are you, sweetie?' I called out loud. There was no answer. Jessie would not be the type of person to not answer. I called again.

The second time, there was a noise that came from the doorway in the wall. I Investigated the noise further, still calling Jess. Then I saw her up against the wall by the door. There was a child shining a torch for me to see. She must have been about six or seven at most, but her hair was too long for a child of her height. Her ponytail was like it was hanging down in the mud as she walked towards me. The poor little girl dissolved into tears and although I didn't know her, my maternal instincts kicked in and I cuddled her.

'It's okay, sweetheart.' I soothed. 'I don't know how or when but will find your mum and dad and get you back to them.' But even as I hugged this child and reassured her, I felt something in my hand that freaked the hell out of me and caught me cold. Not only was her hair too long. Her clothes looked familiar, and they were way too big for her. It was as though she had shrunk. She slipped out of her leggings and her blouse hung loosely around her.

'Becky,' she said softly, confirming my fears that she knew me. 'Don't you dare dob me into my Mum and Dad.'

Stepping back from her a little, my head spun and my heart pumped fear through my veins. That strange witch girl said that she feared consequences when she saved Jessie's life. Her fears had come true, and it was confirmed by the identity badge pinned onto the left side of her top. There was a smiling photograph of Jessie underneath it the read. 'Jessica L. Reynolds.'

Sharon

Things go around in circles. I never knew my mother or my father and didn't want my daughter to end up the same as me. I was in and out of foster care for most of my childhood, and I never really settled with any of my would-be parents.

My most recent foster parents were a couple who I lived with for a while after my daughter was born and removed from my care by my social worker. By my social worker .... I mean her father, the guy who kept telling me he loved me and raped me in my bed at the children's home when I was barely fifteen.

The fucking bastard had a family. A wife and two kids and he never had any intention of leaving them. In fact, when I fell pregnant, he even had the gall to personally arrange to have my child taken away claiming that I refused to tell people who the father was.

He left his job, and he took her away from me, saying that he would make sure I never saw her again. As soon as I was old enough to get out of care, I was looking for my little girl. Once it became clear I was not going to find her, I will admit that I was far from a good role model with my alleged ways.

I played up to my reputation and made up most of the rumours. I probably wrote a lot of this stuff in part two. None of it was true though, as I might have already said. It was just a persona I put on to stop people getting close and finding out what a wreck I really was. Although I think most people knew I wasn't what I professed to be.

At the time we were all sitting there with our arms bound together back-to-back, there was nobody to explain to us what was going on? How or why, we were there or who these people were, where or how they were doing what they were doing.

I thought about what the girl to my right had said when she called me Mum. She really thought I was her mum and I really had thought she was Amber. Whatever twisted shit was going on, there were clearly two of everyone somehow in this twisted dream.

What the real Amber had done in handing herself in to these people was the stupidest, bravest, most selfless act I had ever imagined.

If it turned out that that young lady was my daughter, then I was the proudest and saddest mother in the world.

I didn't want to look at Mike's dead body which was still hanging from my arm.

It seemed to be an hour, but it might only have been 10 minutes. When suddenly we were all lifted to our feet by the force that was holding us together.

That is when the woman with red hair emerged into the centre of the group carrying a screaming baby, and there were gasps of fright as she raised herself above the crowd, floating twenty feet in the air.

Her voice boomed as though she was speaking into a microphone that we could not see.

'My people, our time has come.' She announced in a calm voice as the crowd around us roared. 'It's been a long, long, time. For Four hundred years our people have hidden in the shadows. Sheltering from the sight of those who we were born to destroy, the human vermin.'

Her voice grew in volume. 'Many of us myself included even at Four Hundred years old are still not old enough to remember the days before we were stripped of our powers.... Tonight, we raise our master. Tonight, we join forces with ourselves from other dimensions and with that power, we will bring back the master. He and he alone will grant us the power to kill once more and finish the job as we please.'

She paused for a second, conjuring a handkerchief from the air with ease and a look of slight laughter on her face. 'Do excuse me everyone.' She grinned. 'It seems that our little spell to give all the strong people terrible colds to weaken them has…. Ah ah Achooo…. Achooo Achooo'

The crowd of magical people burst out laughing as she recovered from her sneezing fit, grinning all over her face. She leered and mocked us, mere mortals. She dropped the used handkerchief in the fire below and took a sarcastic bow to the crowd.'

'Now, before the ceremony begins, I would like to mention a few people.' She boomed, 'Like the man and woman who have provided us with this lovely baby, and the pagans who unwittingly built this fire and these Wicca men for us to steal from them.

Without warning, a dazzling light shone all around us to reveal the biggest pile of logs I had ever seen. On top of it were two woven structures, like in the movie Wicca man. May I add you should watch the British original, not the 2006 American remake.

Looking up, I saw something that filled my heart with dread. Inside one of the tall structures at the very top, not screaming or panicking, but just accepting her fate with tears in her eyes, was Amber.

In the other, slightly more panicked as he gazed back at her was Jack. They were reaching across to each other as though trying to hold hands, but they were too far apart.

We watched on in horror as the flames rose, but

Jack and Amber looked at each other bravely. The crowd chanted the words of a spell. Thousands upon thousands of voices singing in perfect time, an eerie, haunting melody. It started as a low hum, but it built and built teasingly. It was as though the purpose of this was to build the fear levels as the flames took hold of the pyre with unnatural speed.

The wordless tune soon became a chant, in words that I could not understand. Some foreign language or one that was so ancient I'd never heard it. Latin, maybe, or some form of old Celtic English. It seemed they were chanting the words of a spell. I didn't know what they were trying to achieve by this but have since learned from others that they believed it would wake Satan himself.

Somebody had placed the baby a short distance from the fire. Obviously, they wanted to use the poor child for their spell, just like they were using Jack and

Amber. Surely nobody could willingly give their child over to these people, knowing the baby was going to come to some sort of harm.

The woman with red hair floated in midair in front of the fire as though it could not burn her. She conducted the crowd in their evil chant as though they were the London Philharmonic orchestra becoming ever more animated as though she was having the time of her life.

The flames rose towards Jack and Amber, and the tears poured. We could not hear their screams as my heart thumped in my chest and flames reached ever closer to the small wicca man heads which imprisoned them.

Something in front of the fire distracted me from looking up. The red-headed flying woman had not seen her coming. A figure had reached the front of the crowd. In the light of the fire through the sweat and tears, I saw her. She was very badly injured and yet still alive, but I can't say how.

Her abdomen seemed to have been cut open at the bottom as though she had been given a C section. Yet clearly not by a doctor because there were no doctors out there. Whoever did it had not intended to let her live. Her intestines and some other very vital organs trailing behind her. As she turned to grab the child I saw her face, and I fought every instinct in my body to shout her name. But then I saw four people in black woollen masks coming out of the shadows behind her and found my voice and screamed at the top of my lungs. 'Kate behind you! Run……'

I saw her pick up the baby and hurry away from the flames. She would never get away and may be dead in seconds but at least she had a few moments to say goodbye to her child before she lost her fight.

To my surprise, the masked figures did not give chase. In-fact they were gathering quietly in the front of the fire and let her pass unchallenged. Her resistance, however, did not last long as more of the wizards simply flashed light out of there hands causing poor Kate to freeze stiff as a board and drop the child at her feet. The two wizards took the baby and placed him or her in front of the fire once more. The dark hooded figures were nowhere to be seen.

Looking at them I had become unaware of more people gathered around us. There was a booming shout that seemed like it came over some sort of public address system. But it was not the witch, it was somebody unseen. I wasn't sure if it was male or female, but it didn't matter.

It spoke loud and clear. 'This is a message from the head of the Freak Society of Great Britain. Anyone who is human prepare to be rescued and close your eyes when instructed and we will try to save you from these….' (He or she said a rude word, I can't type here but it begins with C and ends in S)

The devil worshipers stopped singing as panic hit them. There were confused murmurs from all around us.

The masked figures appeared once more at the centre of the crowd, in front of the fire. There were more of them among the crowd, who were seemingly undoing their robes. Once they seemed ready to throw them off, they all grabbed their masks in unison, as though ready to identify themselves.

The witch flying above the fire did not seem at all worried about this change in events. In fact, she laughed all over her face as though she thought whatever was going to happen was just a brief passing joke. But as she laughed, her face began to change and so did her hair. She was no longer the redhead beauty; she was young blonde and slightly plump. Almost a slightly tubby version of Amber. She smiled down at us all and said calmly. 'They didn't even realise their own leader had been replaced by an imposter! Look away… Ready ladies? in Three, Two, One….'

I looked away just in time as the masked figures stripped themselves bare to a cry of. 'FREAKS TO THE RESCUE.'

Unfortunately, whoever they were, they were too late to save my brave daughter.

In front of my eyes, the flame engulfed the wicca men. Still unable to move. I looked up to see the flames take hold of Amber, while Jack, who had not yet been reached by them, looked on in horror, desperately trying to save her somehow. But nothing could be done. I would never get to find out if she was my child. She was cooked and burned to ashes in front of my eyes.

Amber

So, Sharon saw me die. But I'm not dead I'm alive twenty years later. How might you ask?

From my section earlier in the book you may have understood the situation. The plan was that Jenny would take my place and she would pretend to be me burning. You might have thought it was all her. That she stood up to that woman in my place and stabbed her then took my place in the Wicca man to fool them. But she couldn't be because that red-headed woman was her in disguise. But that was not part of the plan, and I can only assume it was the wrong Jenny. I now know there were two of her.

However, after she shot off into the sky—I believe to save Charlie, then Jessie and Becky—she must have been distracted by something else because she never took my place. That was really me and the real Jack burning up there in those Wicca men.

The flames were real. The pain was real. And me being cooked alive was real. How did I escape death again? How am I alive and pregnant Twenty years later?

Join us for the conclusion of our story in Volume Four A chaotic mess where will conclude our story................ Hopefully.

Derailed and dispersed four, A chaotic mess. out now